MY REDEMPTION

Boston Doms, Book 7

JANE HENRY
MAISY ARCHER

Published by Blushing Books
An Imprint of
ABCD Graphics and Design, Inc.
A Virginia Corporation
977 Seminole Trail #233
Charlottesville, VA 22901

©2017
All rights reserved.

No part of the book may be reproduced or transmitted in any form or by any means, electronic or mechanical, including photocopying, recording, or by any information storage and retrieval system, without permission in writing from the publisher. The trademark Blushing Books is pending in the US Patent and Trademark Office.

Jane Henry and Maisy Archer
My Redemption

EBook ISBN: 978-1-61258-336-5
Print ISBN: 978-1-64563-165-1
v2

Cover Art by ABCD Graphics & Design
This book contains fantasy themes appropriate for mature readers only. Nothing in this book should be interpreted as Blushing Books' or the author's advocating any non-consensual sexual activity.

Chapter 1

"Tell me the story again," Diego Santiago demanded, staring dispassionately at the man tied to a chair in front of him. That man, otherwise known as Ricky Hernandez, slumped against his bindings and gasped a shuddering breath against ribs that were definitely bruised and possibly broken.

"It's like I told you, Padre," the man pled. One of his brown eyes was swollen shut, but the other watched Diego with a sad, wary gaze, knowing that Diego held the man's life in his hands. "The girl was locked up in the cell, just like she was s'posed to be. I was sitting in the hall watching TV. She musta come up behind me, knocked me out, and took off!"

Diego clasped his arms loosely behind his back and paced in front of Ricky's chair as if he were considering this information. He purposely kept the corners of his lips turned up in a slight smile, as though nausea and rage weren't burning a hole in his gut, and his entire right hand wasn't swollen and throbbing from the punishing blows he'd already delivered. In Salazar's crew—or was it *Santiago's* crew now that Diego had been in charge for the past six months? *Jesus*. There was an idea that would have his *Mamá* turning over in her grave—appearances were everything.

He lifted his gaze and surveyed the men who had arranged themselves in a loose circle around Ricky's chair. More than a dozen of them returned his stare, all armed to the teeth and in various stages of inebriation, from stone-sober Banyon to completely-shitfaced Marco, but not a single man moved or spoke. All of them were completely transfixed on the scene.

They weren't happy at the sight of one of their own, a man they considered their brother, receiving his punishment. There but for the grace of God, and all that shit. But there was a grim acceptance about them. Until this morning, if anyone had aimed so much as a disrespectful *word* in Ricky's direction, let alone a violent blow, these men would have thrown down without qualm. But now, Ricky had committed a crime against them, and they'd bear witness to his beating with the same stoicism.

Growing up in this neighborhood, Diego had quickly learned that justice did *not* involve the police, let alone a trial with a robed judge and pricey lawyers. Here, justice was immediate, brutal, and often fatal. Betrayal was the highest crime of all, and there were no loopholes or technicalities that would let you skate once you were caught.

Which is why you're fucking lucky you haven't been caught, he thought wryly. Then he quickly locked that thought away and focused on Ricky once more.

"I want to believe you, Ricky," he lied. "But I'm having trouble here. The girl was in a locked cell, cuffed to a bed." He swallowed down his revulsion as the scene flashed in his mind. "And you want me to believe that she somehow managed to uncuff herself, unlock her cell, *hit you over the head*, and then drag your sorry ass back into the cell and lock you up? Is the girl a fucking magician? Hmm?"

He took a step closer and tilted his head to look at Ricky, who remained silent. "No, *amigo*, she's not. So, here's what I think happened." He smiled, and let his voice turn friendly. Just a couple of buddies, just a pleasant discussion. "I think *you* were fucking horny last night. How many times have I told you that your dick was gonna get you in trouble?" He shook his head in what might have passed for fond exasperation in any other circumstance. "I think you decided that you were gonna have a taste."

Ricky swallowed. "No, I—"

"Ah-ah-ah," Diego interrupted, shaking his head but smiling once again. "Who's the guy who's always bitching about how stupid it is that we transport pussy, but I don't let you sample the goods?"

Ricky's one good eye slid shut. "Me," he admitted, defeated.

"Uh huh. So, last night, you unlocked the girl's cell, and freed her from her cuffs. Then you fucked her, and in the process of *that*, she managed to escape. Sound about right?"

"I-I didn't *free* her," Ricky protested. Somewhere behind Diego, one of the guys snorted. Ricky was looking for that technicality, that loophole that didn't exist. Poor bastard. "And I didn't get to fuck her. I don't know how she hit me. I—"

"No, *estúpido pedazo de mierda*, you just went inside the cell, with your fucking keys on you, whipped your cock out, and let her get the jump on you." Diego took a step forward and reached out his left hand, grabbing Ricky's hair and yanking the man's head back. "*Am I missing anything?*"

A sob erupted from Ricky's throat. "*Padre*. Boss. I swear… Her hands were still tied. I don't know how it happened! It was an accident. I didn't mean for her to escape. I didn't—"

"You didn't *mean*? It was an *accident*?" Diego spat. "Was it an accident when you stepped into that cell, *cabrón*? Was it an accident when you defied my very clear orders that you assholes are not to touch these girls?"

Ricky wept openly now. "I'm sorry, Padre. I'm sorry."

Diego's gut twisted and his jaw locked. "Not sorry enough,

Ricky," he decreed. And then he brought his right arm back and forward, crashing his fist into Ricky's jaw. The reverberation of the punch traveled like a shockwave up Diego's arm, and pain radiated from his knuckles to his shoulder. The chair toppled backwards, crashing to the ground. Ricky's head hit the pavement with a dull thud, then he moaned and fell silent.

Diego stared at the motionless man for a moment, his own chest heaving, before turning to Banyon. "Get him up and into the cell. No doctor. And you give him *nothing* for the pain. No meds. No drugs. No booze, not even a beer. Water, if he wakes up. That's it. I want him to feel every second of his pain. This is the price of betrayal. *Entiendes?*"

"*Sí*, Padre," Banyon agreed. He butted Nico with his shoulder, and the two men stepped forward, silently hauling Ricky's chair back up.

"Look hard," Diego told the others. "This is a man who placed his own desires before his allegiance to our crew. This is a man who *fucked up*. I want you all to remember this: when you fuck up, there will *always* be someone who will capitalize on your mistake..." He let his voice get deeper, silkier. "And there will always, *always*, be consequences."

Marco shuddered and several other men averted their gazes. *Message received.* Diego turned on his heel and headed for his office at the rear of the warehouse without another word.

Christ. How had this bullshit become his life?

He shut the office door behind him and snagged the bottle of *aguardiente* from the low, wooden sideboard with his left hand before collapsing into his desk chair. He hadn't allowed himself to get good and drunk since the day he'd learned that Chalo Salazar—his hated enemy, his former boss—was dead. Alcohol had seemed a fitting solution to the tangled morass of emotions that had swamped him then though, and damn if he didn't feel the same way now.

He removed the stopper from the bottle with his teeth, spit it out and took a deep swig, throwing his booted feet up on the desk. He clenched and unclenched his right hand experimentally. *Fuck, that hurt.* Beneath the myriad small scars he no longer noticed, the knuckles of his calloused hands were red and swollen, but he continued the motion, relishing the sensation. He was no stranger to this type of pain, and it rarely lasted as long as he needed it to.

I want him to feel every second of his pain, he'd told his men. *This is the price of betrayal.* And Diego was a lot of things—a criminal, a traitor, an undercover investigator, and a very, very bad man— but he wasn't a *total* hypocrite. His job was to lead this group of men, to keep them as safe as possible in this dangerous profession, even when that meant doling out punishment. But he also accepted his own pain—welcomed it, even—as the price of *his* disloyalty.

Though fuck if he knew who he was supposed to be loyal to these days. He'd been living a double life so long, the lines between Padre the criminal and Diego Santiago the undercover investigator were blurred nearly beyond recognition.

A knock on the door had him looking up in surprise. He'd expected his men to avoid him after this afternoon's little show, lest they call attention to themselves.

"Come in," he instructed, letting his feet fall to the floor. By force of habit, he reached into the back of his jeans for the Ruger he always carried in his waistband, but only remembered too late that his bruised hand was in no shape to be clutching a piece.

Fortunately, when the door opened, the head that poked inside was a friendly one.

"I keep telling you, you need to carry in the front," Tomás said in amusement, closing the door behind him and taking a chair in front of Diego's desk without waiting for an invitation. "You lose precious seconds in a fight if you've gotta wrestle that thing out of the back of your pants, *hermano*."

He was tall and lean, like Diego himself, and when both men wore jeans, dark t-shirts and their hair pulled back into short queues, as they did today, it was easy to see why some people thought they were blood relatives as well as brothers in arms. Given Diego's father's reputation with the ladies back in the day, Diego figured it was a good possibility.

Diego put the gun down in front of him, rolling his eyes as he kicked his feet back up on the desk and took another deep drink from the bottle he still held. "Better that than carrying up front and accidentally shooting off my own balls."

Tomás raised one eyebrow. "Oh, I dunno, Padre," he said, deliberately using the nickname Diego had first earned himself years ago, when his priest-like celibacy had become a matter of speculation and mocking among the guys. "It's not like you're using that shit, anyway. What's this, your fourth year *con solo tu mano* for company?"

"None of your fucking business," Diego replied. In actuality, he'd passed that mark some months back. "Worry about your own dick."

Tomás smirked and leaned back in his seat, turning his gaze to the ceiling, but Diego kept his eyes fixed on the man's face. No way had Tomás come back here just to shoot the shit. Not tonight.

Sure enough, before a full minute had passed, Tomás looked squarely at Diego. "You shoulda killed him."

Diego set his teeth together but said nothing.

"Ricky disobeyed, flat out. He put us all at risk," he said, holding up his hands as if to prevent Diego from interrupting, "and more than all that, the man broke your number one rule when he went in that girl's cell, Padre."

"As I recall, you didn't like my rule in the first place," Diego remarked, tilting the bottle to his lips without looking away. The alcohol slid down his throat, the burn not nearly as potent after the third swig.

Tomás shrugged. "Majority of these girls sold themselves into prostitution in exchange for a way across the border. They were turning tricks before they got onto the cargo ships, and they'll sure as hell be turning tricks when we take them wherever they're going. Do I think it's stupid that you want us to stay hands-off while they're here? Sure. But it don't matter what I think."

"You don't get hooked on your own product," Diego said, repeating the rationale he'd been using since the day he took over the organization. "Chalo had that rule back when we ran drugs for the cartel, because he knew that users take risks that endanger all of us. Same shit goes with these girls as Ricky just demonstrated."

"So you said," Tomás agreed. "But you're not hearing me, Padre. *It don't matter what I think.* And it don't matter what Banyon or Juancho or Robby or Marco or Ricky think, neither. From your first day running this show, you told us we don't touch the girls we transport, and you told us what would happen if we did. Now, Ricky's gone and done it, and more than that, he let the fucking girl get the drop on him and sneak out of the damn building."

"Which is why I beat the shit out of him."

"You let him off easy."

"I fucking didn't."

"You did! And don't bullshit me, Padre!" Tomás folded his arms across his chest and glared. "You knew exactly what you were doing. What I want to know is *why*. *El Padre* is the meanest motherfucker on the east coast. He doesn't tolerate mistakes, and he doesn't leave loose ends. Why pick *now* as the time to go easy on Ricky? And what are you gonna do about the girl? She heard our names. She knows our faces. Now we're all in jeopardy and El Jefe is gonna be pissed."

Heart beating way too fast, Diego set the bottle on the table, put his boots on the floor, and leaned forward. "You questioning the way I run this organization now, Tomás? You think you could do better? You wanna deal with El Jefe yourself? Make your own rules? Huh?"

The other man's eyes widened, and he held up his hands in protest. "No! No, man. Jesus. You took a knife for me two years back. I had your back when shit went sideways with the Locos. I've always supported you. *Fuck.* I just want to understand."

"You don't understand *shit*, Tomás. The girl is *gone*. Running around the damn city trying to find her is just gonna call more attention to us. Our contacts at the police will alert us if the girl makes a report. And *I* will handle El Jefe when he calls." He gritted his teeth. He was not looking forward to that phone call one little bit. "Now I suggest you get out of my office before I start wondering if Ricky is the only one who needs punishment," Diego added softly.

Tomás staggered to his feet angrily. "I don't get you, man. I thought we were friends. I thought you respected me."

Diego's smile sharpened as he delivered the killing blow. "You said it yourself, Tomás. *It don't matter what you think.*" Then he averted his eyes so he didn't have to see the other man throw open the door and slam it shut behind him.

Fuck, fuck, fuck.

Diego dropped his elbows to his knees and ran his fingers through his hair, making the strands fall around his face though his right hand ached in protest. His beating of Ricky had been thorough and brutal, but he'd known there would be some, like Tomás, who'd expect him to do even more, to make an example of Ricky's deliberate defiance, lest others start to question his authority. In this arena, death would be considered a fair consequence for such a blatant insubordination.

But then, his men didn't realize it was *Diego, himself* who had let the girl free, and *Diego, himself* who had been working for the authorities for almost as long as he'd been a part of this organization. Yeah, he'd punished Ricky—and given that the asshole had been attempting to rape the captive girl this morning before

Diego stepped in, Diego had even found some pleasure in the beating. But how could he kill Ricky for his betrayal when Diego had been the one to break the ultimate rule?

Fuck, he thought again, reaching for the bottle and the sweet oblivion it would bring. *How the hell did I let things get this far?*

Not all of it had been his choice, not in the beginning. He hadn't planned to join Chalo's gang, any more than he'd asked to watch his younger brother get murdered in front of him. Both of those things had been a twist of fate, a shitty hand that life had dealt him. So when he'd stumbled into *Inked* all those years ago, drunk and grieving, begging the first tattoo artist he'd met to inscribe Armando's name on his chest above his heart, it had seemed like a balancing of the scales when the tattoo artist had asked him his story and offered him a way out, a way to make amends.

But if his first meeting with Alexander "Slay" Slater had been fate, everything after that had been Diego's own fucking decision, and he had nobody to blame but himself. *He* had decided to turn traitor and inform on Chalo's crew to Slay's band of operatives and, through them, to the FBI. *He* had been the one who'd dreamt up some fairy tale where that evil asshole, Salazar, would be behind bars, Diego's family would be safe, and Diego could stroll off into the sunset to live his life far away from Boston.

As though anything in Diego's life could ever be that easy.

He'd never envisioned the months he'd planned to stay undercover stretching into years and years. He'd never dreamt that when Salazar finally died, Diego would have to assume Salazar's position in order to gain intel on the next guy up the criminal food chain, El Jefe. He'd never considered that "Salazar's crew" would become his own men—men who'd saved his ass, men he felt responsible for in a fucked up way. He hadn't conceived of the choices he'd have to make and the actions he'd have to take to keep his cover intact. And God knew, he'd never imagined that he'd have to sacrifice any possible future with the only woman he'd ever wanted to call his own.

He'd pulled out his phone before he'd even processed what he was doing, and unlocked it, flipping to the password-protected directory where he kept the most precious information he'd obtained in all the time he'd spent undercover... and then he scrolled through picture after picture of Nora Damon.

The first shot was one he'd taken years ago, back when she was just a teenager, long before he'd ever entertained a thought of her as anything but a funny kid. She'd been stomping around her mom's living room like a pint-sized blonde Hulk, ready to smash Diego, Salazar, and the rest of the crew, including Roger Collier, the asshole dating her mom, who'd invited them all over to party in the first place. Diego had only been maybe twenty-five then, brash and stupid, a newly minted member of Slay's crew, full of anger at the world and Chalo Salazar in particular, but even then there had been something about Nora's spirit that had amused the hell out of him and roused protective instincts he hadn't known he possessed.

The images he didn't have saved on his phone were the ones that truly burned in his mind—Diego helping Slay rescue Nora when Roger had abducted her, and making sure Roger was dealt with *permanently* after the fact.

Next came the family pictures he'd received in texts over the years from Slay and his friend Matteo Angelico—family shots from Thanksgivings and Christmases, weddings and baptisms. Events he'd been invited to, as Slay and Matt had seemed to unofficially adopt Diego into their little family a while back, but which Diego could never attend.

When the first few pictures had rolled in, Diego had found himself scouring each one for Nora's shining blonde hair and big brown eyes, smiling at the sight of her smile. Later, he'd hoard the details the others would drop about her. "Nora's a firecracker," Matteo might grumble. And "She's going to be a social worker at *Centered*, the women's health clinic my sister Elena runs. Saving the world one kid at a time," Slay might brag. Diego would file that information away, each a piece of the fascinating puzzle that was Nora. He wasn't sure at what point his fascination with her had become something other than amusement and affection for the girl she'd been, and had turned into something that burned hot and deep for the woman she'd become. It hardly mattered anyway.

He flipped to his last picture of Nora, one taken just over a year ago at her college graduation. This was a shot he had taken, standing off to the side as she'd received her diploma, his presence undetected and, at least by Nora, unwanted. He smirked as his eyes traced the image of her face. Though she was one of the few people on earth who knew the truth about the reasons for his continued involvement with Salazar's organization, she'd never quite believed that he was the white-knight Slay painted him to be.

Nora was wise that way.

His hands were proverbially dirty now. Bloody. And although the pictures sometimes reminded him of a future he could never have, he couldn't bring himself to delete them. Somehow, remembering that she was alive and safe gave him a reason to keep going. Despite her anger and her mistrust, she'd been his to protect from the first moment he'd laid eyes on her.

That was why, when he'd unexpectedly come back to the warehouse last night and spotted the girl in the cell—a girl with the same golden hair and petite frame as Nora —screaming in terror as Ricky groped her, Diego hadn't stopped to consider the risks or the consequences. He'd grabbed his Ruger from his waistband and cracked the butt into Ricky's skull like it was the easiest thing in the world. And then he'd grabbed Ricky's keys and freed the girl, gathering her into his arms and stepping over the unconscious man as he'd personally escorted her from the building.

"Hush, honey," he'd murmured to her as she'd sobbed silently. "You'll be safe now. I'll make sure of it." And he'd delivered her to the one place, the one *person*, he trusted to protect her: Nora Damon. He'd called Slay and notified him of the situation, then dropped the girl off at *Centered* before dawn.

He locked his phone and threw it on the desk, watching as it slid into the half-full liquor bottle with a hard *thunk*.

His life was a chaos of deception and divided loyalties, of brotherhood and dishonor and broken trust, of *sin* upon *sin* upon *sin* that was somehow supposed to be magically absolved from his soul when they finally found El Jefe and brought his organization to its knees. But what about the girls who passed through this warehouse every week? Did *they* understand, as he and his men transported them from one hellish existence to another, that he couldn't free every one of them, because he was here for a greater purpose, to bring down an even larger criminal, and he couldn't blow his cover?

Should he have killed Ricky today? Would that have been the "right" thing to do? Ricky was no saint, after all, and his death might have earned him added respect and trust from El Jefe, which would further Slay's investigation. Killing Ricky would have stabilized his crew, as Tomás had indicated, and cemented Diego's position as their leader. But at what fucking cost?

Right didn't seem black and white anymore; justice was a riptide that swept up the innocent along with the guilty, and Diego didn't have much of his soul left to bargain with.

His hand reached for the bottle on the desk, but at the last second he changed his mind, grabbed his keys and pushed himself to his feet instead. He didn't need alcohol or anything to dull the pain. He needed a moment of clarity, a second of peace. He needed to see Nora's smile, to know that at least one thing in this fucking world was still pure and true.

And just this once, he was going to let himself have what he needed.

DIEGO WAS LOSING HIS MIND. He'd figured that out halfway here, but he'd come anyway, his need to see Nora overwhelming every rational objection. He had to laugh at himself because, of the many things he had done—and that list was long and incriminating—he'd never imagined he'd stoop to actual stalking. Yet here he was, sitting on a wooden bench in the park across the street from *Centered*, shivering in the chilly October twilight, his long-range binoculars in hand, watching as the people on the other side of the brightly-lit picture windows laughed and chatted their way through some kind of coffee hour and playgroup.

He did make a mental note to tell Slay that they needed to make this place more secure—maybe make sure that there was a man guarding the place after dark, or some shit—because if *he* could sit here and watch the ladies through the window, someone with a darker intent could as well.

He saw Elena, Slay's sister, with her toddler daughter strapped to her back in one of those sling things, making her way around the large room, her black hair bouncing each time she stopped to share a smile or a quiet word with the younger children as they played. He watched as Slay's wife, Allie, who was heavily pregnant, wrapped a comforting arm around an older lady and nodded at whatever the woman was saying. And he saw pretty, dark-haired Grace, who'd recently married Slay's friend Donnie, sitting at a child-sized table drawing something with crayons, encouraging the teenager opposite her to draw as well. This was the sight that arrested him and made his heart squeeze painfully, because the teenaged girl sitting at the table—a girl who couldn't have been more than fourteen and looked even younger, was the very same girl he'd delivered here last night.

She already looked light years better than she had the last time he'd seen her. She was clean and warmly dressed, with her light hair pulled back neatly from her face. But Diego noticed that although Grace kept up a steady stream of chatter and seemed to pause as if expecting the girl to speak, the girl never looked up from the table in front of her, and she never spoke a word. Not a big surprise. The girl's face was pinched and drawn into the perpetually anxious look of someone who's seen too much too young, and Diego felt the contrary urges to enfold the kid in a hug, and to destroy the monsters who'd landed her in his warehouse in the first place.

Grace stood and smiled a goodbye, quickly resting a hand on the girl's shoulder as she took her leave. She pretended not to notice the way the girl flinched at her touch.

Fuck. Diego squeezed his eyes shut. He knew logically that he wasn't the one who'd put that fear in the girl's heart, but he couldn't help the guilt that churned in his belly. How many girls had been harmed on his watch? How many had he failed to save?

Shoulda stuck to the bottle tonight, Santiago. There's no peace for you here. But when he opened his eyes, prepared to leave, Nora appeared.

That blonde hair, those curves, that serene smile. Diego soaked it all in like he'd been thirsty for years.

Unlike Grace, Nora didn't make any attempt at physical contact or small talk with the child at first. In fact, it didn't seem as if they spoke at all. Nora simply took the seat Grace had vacated, and began sketching on a sheet of paper. The little one gave Nora a wary glance, but when Nora made no comment, she looked back down, and some of the tension in her small shoulders seemed to loosen.

Diego smiled. Firecracker though she could be, Nora seemed to understand that sometimes a silent, supportive presence could be more meaningful than any number of words. Another puzzle piece about this woman that he filed away.

Inside the pocket of his jeans, his phone vibrated. *S Calling*

Even though he knew better, he couldn't help that his heart leapt every time Slay's name appeared, that some small part of him always hoped *this* would be the call that said they had enough evidence to take down El Jefe.

With a sigh, Diego glanced once more at Nora and the girl, then stood and walked a distance away, pulling up the hood of his sweatshirt against the cold breeze.

"Evenin', bro," Diego answered, using their established code. An English greeting meant it was safe to speak freely, Spanish meant Diego wasn't alone.

"Diego, man, how's it going?" Slay's voice was quiet and calm. No news, then. It was ridiculous to feel disappointed about that when he should have been used to it by now.

"Livin' the life, brother. You know how it is. Haven't heard from you in a bit," Diego said, leaning his back against the trunk of a wide oak tree whose discarded leaves littered the ground around him. "How's the fam? What are you up to?"

"Family's good! Great, even. Charlie got first prize at his science fair. Twins haven't burned the house down yet, although Lex keeps trying to bench-press the dog and Mase keeps coloring himself with Sharpies so he can look like his Daddy." Slay chuckled. "The usual."

Diego couldn't help but smile. When he'd first met Slay, the man had been a total hardass—a soldier, a dominant, a warrior. But his voice carried a thread of deep contentment these days. He was still the most lethal man Diego knew, but now he seemed to be grounded in something Diego couldn't quite fathom.

"Gonna pick up Allie in a few," Slay continued. "Got a babysitter coming, then we're heading to The Club for a bit. She hasn't been in over a month, and she's been dying to go."

The Club, the BDSM club founded by Elena's husband Blake, was pretty much a staple in the Boston kink scene. Slay had started working security there long after he'd gotten his own security team off the ground, but he'd loved it so much he'd become a part-time Dungeon Master, and was now part-owner. He remembered that Slay had met his wife Allie when she'd been bartending there.

"Dude, Allie's so pregnant she's ready to pop and you're taking her to a club?" Diego teased, only realizing after the fact that Slay might wonder how he'd seen Allie recently enough to know this. Fortunately, Slay seemed to roll with it.

"Brother, we don't go to The Club to drink and dance, ya get me?" Slay replied, making Diego snort. "Though it's been a long time since you've been around, so maybe your memory is failing."

Diego swallowed hard. Oh, his memories of The Club were clear as day, and he replayed them often, though it had been a long time since he'd been there and even longer since he'd allowed himself to take part in even the most platonic demonstrations. He loved dominance, craved the control, but the casual interactions had never satisfied that need. In another reality, one where El Jefe and the cartels didn't exist, he knew he'd have found himself *one* woman and done everything in his power to possess her totally.

"I was calling to invite you to a party, actually," Slay continued when Diego didn't speak. "A fundraiser for *Centered*. It's gonna be out in a field somewhere, with face painting and beanbag tosses and a dunk tank and shit. Allie says it'll be a good way for the donors to interact with the actual women and children their money helps. I'm personally going because Tony's catering."

"A dunk tank? Oh, please tell me Alice convinced you to take a turn!" Diego imagined Slay, soaking wet and sputtering, as some tiny eight-year-old's throw hit its mark. He laughed out loud.

"Whatever, dipshit. It's for fucking *charity*," Slay said as Diego laughed louder. "Who could say no?"

Diego wiped his eyes with the back of his hand. "Oh, God, I can't wait to see the pictures, man."

Slay was quiet for a minute. "Rather you saw it in person for once."

"I can't," Diego said flatly, crossing his arms over his chest to keep warm. "Same reason I can't go to any of the stuff you invite me to. It's not safe. And you know I can't just—"

"Nah. Shut it," Slay interrupted. "You let *me* handle the safety. You think I'd invite you to be around my family if I thought for one second it wouldn't be safe? Fuck that. And I also told you, we could come up with an iron-clad reason why you need to disappear for a day or two. Nobody in your organization would be the wiser. So what's the real reason?"

Diego rolled his shoulders so his head rubbed against the rough bark of the tree as he tried to find a handy excuse, but nothing came to mind.

Goddamn it. It wasn't as simple as Slay tried to make it seem. It *wasn't.* He *had* been around Slay's family a couple of times over the years when it was unavoidable, but he didn't fit with them. He didn't know how to talk politely anymore, or how to let his guard down.

And being around them made him want things he couldn't afford to want.

"I'm worried about you, Santiago," Slay said into the silence, and his voice was as heavy as Diego had ever heard it. "This assignment… It was never supposed to go down like this. You were never supposed to be in this long. And I know you won't admit it, but it's gotta be fucking with your mind."

Once again, Diego struggled to respond. *Nah, man. I'm chill. I just do despicable shit all day, and then build friendships with criminals over beers at night. No worries.*

Yeah, right.

"Been talking to Matteo, and I think it's time to pull you out,"

Slay continued. "And it's not just about you. This week we got a new FBI contact named Darby, some pissant who doesn't know his ass from his elbow, but seems bound and determined to..."

What the fuck? "Pull me?" The words came out louder than he'd intended.

"Yeah. End the investigation and get you out," Slay elaborated, but Diego had already understood what he meant, he just couldn't believe he was hearing it.

"No fucking way."

"Dammit, be reasonable, man," Slay began.

"You were the one, Slay," Diego told him in a furious whisper. "You were the one who told me, all those years ago, that *this* was the way I would atone for the shit I did, *this* was the way I'd make things right for Armando. And now you wanna pull me before I can do that?"

"Jesus, no! Is that what you thought? You were a *kid* then, Diego. You needed an enemy to face down, a battle to fight, so I gave you one. You didn't wanna hear me talk about how you had nothing to do with Armando's death, and how you weren't responsible for the things Chalo forced you to do when he threatened your family. I never believed for a single minute that you had anything to atone for. You wanted vengeance, and I wanted to help you get it, but not like this. Not if it means losing yourself."

Oh, fuck. Diego felt moisture behind his eyes, and he blew out a harsh breath. "Yeah. Well. I'm in it now, Slay. I've got a job to do, and I'm gonna see it through."

Slay sighed. "Yeah. Figured you'd say that. But I'm not letting this shit play out for too much longer, you hear me? You made your choices, I respect them, but I'm not gonna let you kill yourself in some fucked up attempt to do the right thing. I love you, brother." Slay paused, and Diego heard him inhale sharply before he continued. "But I'm pretty sure you don't even know what the right thing is anymore."

Diego shook his head and sighed. The man was fucking psychic when it came to reading people and situations. Diego didn't know why it even surprised him at this point. "I hear you," he replied.

Slay was silent so long that Diego wondered if he'd hung up, and when he spoke again, he did so slowly, like he was pulling the words from someplace deep.

"I don't… I don't talk about some of what I had to do, back when I was in the service, and even after that. I worked at Black Box—before I worked with Blake, I mean—and they did some pretty twisted shit there, you know?"

"I remember." Black Box was a BDSM club that had been partly owned by Chalo Salazar and Salazar's cousin, an arrogant asshole who'd called himself Marauder. Consent and legality had been nebulous concepts at Black Box.

"I thought my presence there was a good thing, like I was preventing the *worst* of the crimes from happening, and I thought maybe I could help someone. But… the scales never seemed to balance. For a long time after that, I felt lost."

"Yeah," Diego whispered. The cold wind whipped the leaves around his ankles and had turned his fingers to ice, but he gripped the phone tighter.

"That was my mess to deal with, right? I mean, my choice, my consequences. So I locked my shit up tight and hid in plain sight. Took on dangerous jobs like that would even the score, then ran away from a good woman who tried to love me because I was worried about what I'd bring down on her."

"Alice?" he asked, stunned.

"Alice," Slay confirmed. "Good thing I pulled my head out of my ass or I would have lost her. Don't let that happen to you."

"Me? The guy they call Padre?" Diego scoffed, deliberately training his gaze away from *Centered*. "I'm not in love with anyone, man. I'm clear."

"Huh. Nobody special?"

Goddamn the psychic asshole. "Nobody," Diego lied.

"You're sure about that?"

"Uh, yeah. Pretty sure, Slay," Diego said. "And I think I'd know."

"All right, bud. If you say so. But, hey, next time you wanna spend an hour sitting in front of *Centered* watching *nobody special*, maybe wear a heavier jacket. October nights in Boston are no joke."

Across the park, Diego watched a tall, broad figure step out of the deep shadows formed by another stand of trees. In the yellow glow of the streetlight, he saw the figure throw him a mocking salute. "Remember, I'm always watching, Santiago. Later."

Diego snorted. He watched Slay jog across the street and up the steps to Centered, then slid his own phone back in his pocket. He began his solitary journey back across town, but somehow felt less alone than when he'd arrived.

Chapter 2

Nora Damon leaned up against the desk at *Centered*, trying to keep her shit together.

Earlier in the night, she'd allowed herself to indulge in the age-old "woe is me," a luxury she rarely allowed herself. There was something about seeing Elena, with her sweet little baby strapped to her back, and Alice, waddling around heavily pregnant, that caused Nora to grow wistful. Everyone she loved was either happily married or close to it. Even Grace, who'd gotten a parting kiss from her husband Donnie, made Nora a little jealous. It didn't help that her inner circle of friends wasn't a random assortment of college-aged couples, but couples who'd forged their bonds through trials and blessings, all dominants and submissives she'd befriended who were members of The Club. These couples were committed: the women fiercely loyal and the men devoted.

As the lone single girl, being around such relationships sometimes set her off kilter. Though the past few years she'd done nothing but dedicate herself to completing her degree in social work and beginning her career, Nora couldn't help but long for what her friends had. She'd dated a few guys in college—guys who were as studious as she was, good guys who paid their bills on time and cleaned their cars out before they picked her up, clean-shaven men she should have been proud to date. But they paled in comparison to the gritty, possessive men she'd come to know and love. The relationships her friends and even her sister and brother-in-law had weren't the kind of relationships she'd ever thought she'd want. Growing up with a mother who'd given her power away to any man who'd look twice at her, Nora had always valued her independence fiercely. But recently, she couldn't help but wonder what it would be like to have someone she could lean on, someone she could instinctively trust, someone who would support her when life became too demanding.

Tonight, however, jealous thoughts vanished as she looked upon the girl who sat at the table with Grace. The girl who reminded her eerily of herself, with similar curves and long blonde hair. But those eyes... her fear-filled eyes were nothing like Nora's.

The girl was fucking terrified.

Nora clicked the ballpoint pen in her hand so rapidly, Allie finally put her hand on her arm. "Nora, honey," Allie whispered in her ear, "we're all pissed. We all know something terrible has happened to her. But let's stay calm and get to the bottom of this, yeah?" In the years since Nora had known Allie, she'd seen her learn Slay's "calm, cool, and collected" approach to intense situations. No one could handle a toddler tantrum or screaming baby with as much ease as the Alice-Slay parenting combo, and their approach to intense situations carried over into all areas of their lives. Nora wished she could learn to be as chill.

"We'll have to call the police," Nora whispered back to Allie. "I don't want to do it yet, but something tells me this girl has experienced things we'll need to report." Though the girl wasn't talking to anyone, she seemed to enjoy the company of the group around her, and gravitated toward the art project Grace was orchestrating.

Alice shrugged, frowning, as she leaned back against the desk next to Nora, resting her hand on her swollen abdomen. "Yeah," she said thoughtfully. "But we both know she won't speak if they're here. And because she hasn't actually said a word to us, and has no physical signs of abuse, we don't need to call yet."

Nora nodded. "Of course."

Nora had sat beside the girl for a few minutes before she couldn't take it anymore. Sometimes, her sense of justice and impatience got the best of her. She wanted to throttle whoever had hurt the girl, and she knew she needed to calm the hell down. Now, though, it was time to try to help her, even if it meant she'd spend three hours sitting beside the girl, coloring.

Nora watched Grace interact with her for a while longer, trying to get her to draw, but the girl would have none of it. Grace finally got up and moved away, and Nora took the opportunity to try to reach her. She pushed off the desk, walked over to the table, and sat down. She picked up a piece of paper and began doodling. *Centered* wasn't just a medical facility but a safe haven, a non-profit that focused on offering peaceful sanctuary to women who needed it. They focused on positivity and wellness, and welcomed all visitors regardless of their situations. Because *Centered* was located in the inner city, though, workers often saw victims of severe trauma.

"I'm going to color for a bit," Nora said as if to herself, though she hoped the girl was listening. "It helps me relax sometimes," she said. "Or draw, and doodle." Her hand swept across the page in an arc, outlining a rainbow with fluffy clouds. She picked up a colored pencil and sketched in red, followed by orange and yellow, until she'd colored in the entire rainbow. The girl sat stock still, her hands in her lap, watching Nora. She did not speak, and Nora wondered for a moment if she was even breathing, but a quick glance, and she could see the steady rise and fall of the girl's chest.

"I like to draw," Nora murmured. "Just let my mind wander,

and lose myself in doodling. Some people like Grace are good at it," she said, hoping that if she talked about her co-workers nonchalantly, the girl might feel less threatened. "Grace is *amazing*. Me, I just like to fiddle around. Here, why don't you try?" She pushed a piece of paper and pencil over, half expecting the girl to stay unmoving. But slowly, her little hand, as small as a child's, grasped the charcoal pencil from the assortment in the tin in front of her. The pencil was more suited for sketching, unlike the colored ones Nora fiddled with. In seconds, the girl sitting beside her had drawn large blocks. Nora tried to pretend she was keeping her cool, not watching in rapt attention at what transpired in front of her. The blocks took on different shapes, some shaded, stacked beside one another, and after a little while longer, Nora could tell that they were not merely cubes anymore, but block letters.

C-A-M-I-L-A.

"Oh," Nora said, dropping her voice to a whisper as she leaned in closer to the girl. "Is Camila your name?"

Though she still got no response, a quick glance at the girl's face, and Nora could tell she was getting somewhere. The girl's lips turned up, and her frightened eyes had grown hopeful.

Nora continued to whisper. "Very nice to meet you, Camila," Nora said, so low that no one but Camila could hear her. "I want you to know something, honey," she continued, her voice wavering a bit as she blinked back tears that suddenly filled her eyes. "You're safe here with us. No matter what has happened to you, we will take care of you."

Camila closed her eyes briefly before nodding, tapping the pencil in her hand. Not wanting to scare her off, Nora went back to the paper. The staff at *Centered* had discovered the benefits of therapeutic art classes, and even those who worked at *Centered* enjoyed taking part. Grace would lead them through techniques that helped relax them, free painting or drawing, even working with clay or beads. There was something about creating with their hands, in a safe place, that helped their clients relax.

"Sometimes," Nora said, looking at her paper and not at Camila, "I like to draw things that calm me. It doesn't always come out the way it is in my mind, but I don't really care. Stick figures can be symbolic."

To Nora's surprise, Camila laughed then, a soft giggle Nora could barely hear. Hiding a smile, Nora continued to draw. She sketched a rectangular bar and wrote *Hershey's* across the front, coloring it in deep browns before she drew a picture of a coffee cup with a swirl of steam at the top. Next, she drew music notes, and beside that, a crude stack of books. "These are the things I relax with," she murmured, darkening the edges of the drawing, shading a bit here and there. She took a deep breath before speaking again. "Maybe you'd like to draw something like this, too. Something that makes you feel safe."

Camila stared at her pencil thoughtfully for a minute, running one finger along the smooth edge of the barrel. As she fidgeted with the pencil, her lips turned down thoughtfully. Had Nora somehow hit a nerve with her? Not breathing, careful not to move too fast. Nora continued to draw on her own paper, little by little sketching stars and hearts and flowers in a border around her picture of things that made her feel safe. She took the paper and looked at it, forgetting for a minute that Camila sat beside her. She folded the paper and tucked it into her pocket, before she realized with a start that Camila had begun to draw.

She no longer drew blocks or shadows, but the oval shape of a face, first one line then another, softening the look, before she sketched dark eyes beneath heavy brows, and a thin nose. The drawing was symmetrical, and already anyone who looked at it could tell this was no mere stick figure or an amateur drawing. The girl could *draw*. Angled cheekbones and a full mouth, severe lines around the eyes that made the face appear serious and thoughtful. Nora watched in rapt attention as Camila continued.

Was it her mother? A sister, perhaps? It was hard to tell without the hair in place, but with another flourish of the pencil, a scruffy beard appeared along the jawline. Her father, maybe? A brother? But then the drawing really began to take form, and Nora had the odd feeling that she knew those eyes.

Did she?

Her breath caught in her throat, the hair at the back of her neck standing on end, as Camila's pencil flew over the skull now, adding hair. Nora knew what it would look like before it took form on the page. Dark hair, so long he could tuck it behind his ears, framing his face, the hard angles of his jaw in sharp contrast to the shocks of jet black hair.

Draw something that makes you feel safe, Nora had said.

She stared at the unmistakable face of Diego Santiago.

THANK GOD EVERYONE else in *Centered* had been busy doing something else. One of the kids had knocked over a cup of water used for painting, and the volunteers and workers were busy cleaning it up. Nora got to her feet and snagged Camila's drawing. "I'll put this safe in my office, so no one spills anything on it, okay?" she said to Camila, who only nodded.

She tucked it into her pocket before anyone else could see. The drawing was so vivid, so lifelike, Nora could almost hear Diego scolding her from the paper. Was it right to hide this evidence from Alice, Elena, and Grace? They'd want details. Nora told herself it was just as well that she kept this to herself right now, because the last thing anyone needed to do was worry, and any sort of reaction from anyone else could scare the girl. Nora had made more progress with her than anyone else had. She didn't want to scare Camila back into her shell.

Diego Santiago. *God.*

She needed to see him, to understand why he made Camila

feel safe, to find out why Camila knew him at all and, she wasn't too proud to admit to herself, but because some part of her craved to see him in person, in the flesh rather than in her dreams too.

"We're going to get something to eat, and tonight I'll arrange for a place for the girl to stay," Alice said softly, low enough that only Nora could hear.

"Her name is Camila," Nora whispered, leaning in so Alice could hear her as she discreetly showed Alice the block letter drawing.

"Ah, is it? What a lovely name," Alice mulled, her hand at her chin as she looked at Camila, who stood apart from the others now, watching them clean up.

"She drew it," Nora said.

Alice nodded. "I'm glad she opened up to you. She must like you, or trust you."

Trust.

Guilt churned in Nora's stomach. Didn't she trust her friends? No one but Nora and Camila needed to know that Diego Santiago had somehow been in Camila's life before the girl came to *Centered*. Was he somehow related to her? Nora did the math quickly in her mind. Diego would be about thirty years old, and this girl was a young teen. He *could* be her father, but it wasn't very likely. It was much more likely he had something to do with her rescue.

Shit.

Feigning a yawn, Nora stretched her arms over her head. "I'm exhausted," she said to Alice. "I need to get some rest tonight. I've got a full day tomorrow. Do you and Elena need help arranging for a place for Camila to stay?"

Alice shook her head, her gaze still focused on Camila. "Of course not, honey," she said. "She's in good hands. Tomorrow, maybe we make a little more progress, but at least we've got something tonight."

They sure did. "Okay, then," Nora said, smiling brightly at Camila, and waving her hand. Camila waved back, but her eyes still looked haunted.

"You're in good hands," Nora said to the girl, who looked to Elena and Alice, and nodded. "I'll see you tomorrow." A part of her felt guilty for leaving when the girl was still so shaken, and she was really the only one who had made a connection with her, but she had to get to Diego. If she was going to make any headway in figuring out what the hell had scared this girl, she needed to see him, *now*.

She slung her bag over her shoulder and grabbed her phone, scrolling through the text messages. She had one from her sister Tessa, asking if she could babysit the following night. She'd call her later. She didn't even want to call or text Tess, as if somehow Tessa's big sister intuition would know that Nora was about to do something very, very dangerous.

Sometimes it was better to keep things to yourself.

THOUGH IT WAS A BEAUTIFUL EVENING, Nora's stomach churned and her head pounded. Just coming back to the wharf did strange things to her that even the cool night air could not soothe. Amidst the leaves, tinted golden yellow and deep rust, crimson and fiery red, she could smell the salt air, *feel* that she was near the wharf. Here, where Diego Santiago had rescued her from the clutches of her mother's sick boyfriend, Roger, all those years ago.

Her fingers tapped against the steering wheel as she drew closer to the warehouse. What would it be like to look at those sterile walls again, the nondescript interior that promised sordid torture to the victims brought to the criminals' lair? Had Camila been inside there? Nora shivered as she took the exit off the highway and headed toward the wharf, following the smell of fish, salty air, and fear.

It had been a night like this one a few years ago when Roger had taken her to the warehouse near the wharf with some crazy plan to dispose of her before she could rat him out to the cops. Nora recalled the moments of stark terror when she'd been tied up and helpless in that cavernous building, surrounded by Roger, Diego, Chalo Salazar, and the other criminals who'd wanted to hurt her. Petrified as she'd been, she remembered also being wildly, irrationally disappointed in Diego.

Diego had been to her mother's apartment numerous times before that night, along with the rest of Salazar's crew, but something about him had set him apart from the idiots he hung around with. Something in his eyes had been warm and kind. He'd never leered at her, commanded her, crowded her, or intimidated her. When one of the assholes had tried to kiss her, Diego had stepped in and provided distraction so that she could get away. He'd winked at her as she scowled at the men in the living room. He'd made her feel *important* in a way that no one, except maybe Tess, ever had before. But Tess didn't have Diego's tall, lean-muscled swagger or his gorgeous dark eyes.

Even though Nora had known better, even at that early age, she'd found herself more than half in love with the man. She'd painted a picture of him in her mind as her white knight, a man who would save her from the constant fear that was pretty much the hallmark of life with her mother. She'd imagined he'd take care of her.

Seeing Diego standing with Salazar at the warehouse, obeying his orders, had shattered Nora's fantasy like glass.

Sure, Diego had beaten the shit out of Roger, and then apparently dealt with him in a more *permanent way*. He'd returned her to her sister and, as everyone from Slay to Tony to Matteo liked to remind her, he'd *saved her*. But none of them had seen the coldness in his eyes as he'd looked at her that night, the way he'd smiled at Salazar, the way he'd joked and laughed with the other men as she'd sat, tied to a chair, wondering if she'd be alive to see the next sunrise. The truth had been absolutely apparent to her, as she'd watched him that night—she wasn't special to Diego, and she never had been. She'd been as delusional as her own mother, falling for a criminal who wanted nothing more than to suck her dry.

That day, she'd hardened her heart to Diego Santiago.

There had been more than a few times over the intervening years when she'd felt herself softening towards him. A few months back, he'd come to Tony's restaurant *Cara*, when Donnie and Grace had needed his help, and he'd looked so damn *tired* that she'd wanted to comfort him. And last month, she'd been walking up the path to Allie's house when Diego had come trotting down the front steps unexpectedly. Their eyes had locked, and for a second Nora had allowed herself to see the warmth that she remembered shining there.

But, did that make him trustworthy? She took a deep breath and steeled her resolve.

There were a billion unanswered questions where Diego was concerned. No one else seemed to find it odd that Salazar had been killed months ago, but Diego still remained undercover. Why would he choose to do that? And how had Camila known his face?

She parked in a dark lot with only a few cars present, about a block from the entrance to the warehouse. Ostensibly, the warehouse imported souvenirs they distributed all over the state, but she was one of the few people outside of Diego's gang members and Slay's special ops guys who knew it was a mere front for Salazar's—and now Diego's—criminal enterprises.

She hesitated for a moment, wondering if Diego would even be here tonight. What if she found only the sick bastards of his crew inside? Maybe it wasn't a good idea to plow into this situation unprepared.

It wouldn't matter whether he was there, if you really believed he was as dangerous as the rest of those criminals, a voice in her head taunted. *But you don't, do you?*

She ignored the voice. Her gut said he'd be here anyway, that tonight she'd face him and get the answers she needed for Camila, and perhaps for herself too.

Determined to get to the bottom of everything, Nora opened her eyes, tucked her bag under her seat, and got out of the car, hitting the door lock button behind her. She shivered from the breeze that came off the water. It was easily ten degrees cooler here than at *Centered*, and she'd left her damn sweatshirt back at the office. Whatever.

Keeping her head down, she marched in the direction of the warehouse, walking so quickly she was almost jogging. When she finally drew close enough to see the comings and goings of the men on the pier, she stood behind a large stack of crates, peering around the corner, hoping to get a glance of Diego. She held her breath as the men she'd know anywhere walked in front of her, talking in low tones to one another, hissing words in Spanish that she didn't understand. She caught a few words here and there, and one phrase they repeated many times. El Jefe.

Was El Jefe Diego? A hefty, dark-skinned man with greasy hair that hung in his eyes stepped out of the door to the warehouse, taking a drag on a cigarette. He inhaled deeply, then lifted his head back and exhaled, wisps of smoke circling the chilly night. Nora watched as man after man went into the warehouse, maybe a dozen altogether, some of whom she didn't recognize. Had Diego's band grown? As she watched, one man turned, and the light of the full moon illuminated the side of his face. She covered her mouth with her hand, stifling a gasp. His face was a mottled assortment of bruises, one eye swollen shut, his lip twice the normal size.

The true dangerousness of the situation finally dawned on

her. What did these men *do*? What the fuck had she been *thinking*, coming here alone?

Shuddering, she rubbed her hands briskly, trying to warm herself, when suddenly a hand covered her mouth, and a voice so close it was practically in her ear spoke. "Colder here than at *Centered*, eh, niña?"

Mustering all her courage, she turned to see the man who spoke to her, her heartbeat slowly returning to normal as she stared at the all-too-familiar, heartbreakingly handsome face of Diego Santiago.

His eyes narrowed on her, his jaw set, his hands planted on his hips. The man was *pissed* as he leaned in closer to her and whispered. "I don't know what the *fuck* you're doing here, but you're going to get back in your car, head home, and pretend you never came. And if you do exactly what I say, I may pretend you never came, too."

Though she'd been thinking the very same thing a minute ago, she'd be damned if she did it because he said so!

"No way," she hissed, "and who the hell do you think you are scaring me like this?"

"I'm the man they call Padre, Nora," he whispered, the low rumble of his voice making the hair at the back of her neck stand on end. "The one in charge here. And if you think I'm scary, you should consider yourself lucky that none of the guys inside found you out here. I'm telling you to get the hell away. You have no business here."

"Maybe I fucking *do* have business here," she said. She wanted to hit him, to *hurt* him, for scaring her, for not being the man she'd imagined him to be all those years ago, for having anything to do with this whole fucking operation to begin with.

His beautiful dark eyes were hot and flared anger as he watched her, and a thought came to her suddenly. *He's too good for this shit. He deserves better.*

She sucked in a breath as realization dawned. She'd been

trembling in fear before Diego had appeared behind her. Now, suddenly, she could stand her ground because she knew it was safe for her to fight. Her heart was recognizing what her mind wouldn't allow her to fully process—that Diego wouldn't let anything harm her, not physically at least. *You want him. You trust him more than you realize.*

The insight pissed her off. She had perfectly good reasons not to trust him, goddamn it! And she certainly didn't want someone so bossy, so controlling! But her thundering heart wouldn't listen to that logic.

He raised a brow, and his lips thinned, turning down at the edges. He skewered her with a severe look, his voice low and husky. "Such a naughty mouth for a little girl." he said softly, arms crossing over his chest, his muscles bulging.

Her breathing stuttered and her panties dampened. *Shit.*

"Where are you parked?" he growled.

Still glaring at him, she nodded her head to the lot where she'd left her car.

"Come with me," he ordered. "*Now.*" Without another word, his large, warm hand wrapped around her upper arm, firm enough that she couldn't get away without a struggle but gentle enough that it didn't hurt, and he marched her toward her car. "You open your mouth, Nora, and the trouble you're in with me gets a lot worse."

"What are you—"

He hissed, and she closed her mouth. *Fine.* She didn't want to get the attention of his crew anyway.

She tried to yank her arm away from him, but he held fast as he marched her along, going so quickly she had to trot to keep up with his long strides. He was a good deal taller than she was, lean and muscular, his limbs moving with fluid grace as he propelled her to the parking lot.

"Go home, Nora," he said, releasing her arm and giving her a little shove toward her car.

She spun around to look at him, furious at his audacity.

"No!" she said, planting her hands on her hips. "I don't go home until I get answers."

His eyes narrowed, and he took a step toward her. "You don't tell me no, little girl." His body and the fury that pulsed from him forced her back a step before his intimidating glare eased slightly. "Jesus, Nora, it isn't safe here. Now get your ass in that car and go home before I'm forced to make you."

"Make me?" she said, throwing her arms up in the air as desire warred with frustration. "What the fuck is that supposed to mean?" His eyes narrowed on hers. "You don't *make* me do anything, Diego. I'm not one of your fucking henchmen. You can't order me around like that."

He took another step toward her so she was forced to take a step backward. "Such a filthy mouth," he growled. "If you were mine, I'd teach you what to do with that mouth."

And just like that, despite her anger, despite the fact that her palm itched to smack his smug, beautiful face, her heart skipped a beat and her belly dipped. God, he was so different from the polite guys she dated in college. She had no idea exactly what he'd do to teach her manners, but her body yearned to know.

No! her mind denied. *It's the cold. It's the loneliness. It's your shared history, and the way that he saved you. It's the fact that he's so fucking hot you can't stand it!*

"Teach me manners?" she spat back at him. "You're not my father, asshole," she said, realizing that she was protesting far too much.

And with that, she somehow hit a nerve. She knew the second she did because he moved so quickly she couldn't breathe, crossing the distance between them in two quick strides as he reached for her, his hand wrapping around the back of her neck, making goosebumps rise along her arms as her eyes widened. His grip firm on the sensitive skin of her neck, he directed her gaze to his.

"You're right," he said in a furious whisper, "I'm not your daddy. But with a mouth like yours, it'd be my pleasure to teach you the manners your daddy should've taught you." His lips turned up in a sneer. "I'd put that beautiful mouth of yours to good use."

She wanted to challenge him, wanted to smack her hand against the wall of his chest, strip off his shirt and run her nails along his naked skin. She wanted to make him hurt, wanted to make him *bleed*.

What was it about this man that caused her to lose complete control of her senses?

"Fuck you," she hissed. And with that, it seemed as if his resolve snapped.

"You think I'm shitting around?" he asked, pushing her back to her car. "I've put bullets in the skulls of thieves and molesters," he growled, pulling her alongside him. "Just today I beat a guy so badly I could have killed him. And you think I wouldn't hesitate to whip your ass for your defiance? To teach you to keep safe and watch your mouth? You don't talk to me that way, little girl." He tried to yank the door open to her car, but it was locked tight.

Her head swam with fury and arousal, the *nerve* of him making her fists clench at her sides and her belly tingle with want.

"Open the goddamned door," he commanded, and her stomach dropped.

Shit.

She swallowed, trying to wrench her arm free from his, but to no avail. "I-I don't have my keys," she said in a little voice. "I-I may have... um... locked them inside."

"*Madre de Dios,* Nora," he growled. He gritted his teeth together and appeared to be thinking before he spat. "Fine, then. You're coming with me. You walk with me, and you don't say a word. I've had enough of this shit. You disobey me, and I'll spank your ass right here. You get me?" And she knew he would.

He was a man who always did what he said. She swallowed, and nodded, all thoughts of a fight fleeting.

She couldn't hear everything the man on the other side said, but she heard the parting words. "*Si*, Padre."

She remained quiet as they finished walking to his car. He beeped his key and the locks clicked open. He yanked open the passenger door, practically shoving her in. She slid onto the seat, as he nabbed the seatbelt and pulled it across her, buckling her in before she could protest. *God!*

He locked and shut her door, jogging over to his side. He sat down in his seat, buckled himself in, shut the door, started the car, and took off so fast, his wheels squealed as they headed toward the exit. She sat in his car, her mind a swirl of emotion. He was so fucking *bossy*.

Then why did heat swirl in her belly, throb between her thighs, and her pussy clench as she thought about his threats to teach her a lesson, to watch her mouth, to spank her ass? She swallowed. The men she knew were dominants, badass alphas who took shit from no one. And though she hadn't witnessed what went on at The Club, she knew her girlfriends were into this. Even Tessa and Tony toyed around with the whole dominance and submission thing. She knew there was... discipline involved at... some level. She knew Slay and Matteo were dungeon masters, and Grace's fiancé Donnie was the primary operator of Club South.

Though they didn't discuss details, she was no dumbass. She knew that the girls were submissives, and that they got spanked. And in her deep, dark fantasies she had to admit, it all sounded kinda hot to her. Still, she'd told herself it wasn't her thing. She didn't like being told what to do. She'd worked too damn hard to get where she was to just hand it all over to some Neanderthal who'd spank her ass if she disobeyed him. Uh uh, no way Jose, not happening.

But now she sat next to Diego as he wove through the traffic of downtown Boston, his jaw set in anger, his last parting words echoing in her ear, she was more turned on than she'd been when her last date had felt her up.

When they moved out of the clustered streets of downtown Boston and onto the highway, he turned to her.

"Tell me why you came," he demanded. "And I'll know if you're bullshitting me."

"Nice to see you, too," she muttered, but he only growled in response.

She sighed. She'd come here to confront him, and there was no point in not telling him, even if she didn't feel like doing whatever the hell he said. "I came because you know something I need to know," she began.

He drove in silence, but raised one questioning brow. "This morning at *Centered*, a girl came in."

Still, he said nothing.

"She won't talk. She's clearly been traumatized, but we don't know the extent of it. She has no visible signs of abuse, so we haven't called the police, but we are hoping we can get her to talk." He nodded.

"And though I can't get her to say anything, I got her to tell me her name. Camila." She paused, watching his reaction. "Ring a bell, Diego?"

His face remained impassive. "Nope. Tell me why you came to the wharf, Nora," he said, his tone growing impatient.

Nora sighed. "So I asked this girl to draw something that made her feel safe. And you know what she drew?"

"Sitting on the edge of my seat over here," he said, his voice dripping with sarcasm.

"She drew you."

He said nothing as he flicked on his directional and got off the highway, but his grip on the steering wheel tightened.

"That doesn't tell me why you came to the wharf."

She blew out a breath. "You're not an idiot, Diego. I came

because I need answers. I need to know why some traumatized little girl was dropped off at *Centered*, and the first person that comes to mind when we talk about feeling safe is you? Come on. You don't want me to give that sketch to the police, do you?" It was a low blow, but she needed to get the information from him.

"Excuse me?" he said, his voice low. She felt the correction in it, and once again her pulse spiked. She swallowed as he continued. "All you told me is that some girl came to *Centered* and drew a guy that looked like me. And now I'm supposed to just give you all the details of an ongoing undercover investigation? How the hell do I know if what you're telling me is true?"

"You think I'm lying?" she said. "Arrrgh!" She groaned out loud, frustrated by this bossy, aggravating man.

He clenched his jaw, pulling down a vacant street and driving swiftly toward a large house at the end of the road. "But I'm not just going to tell you all my shit because some girl drew something that looked like me." He parked in front of the house, and before she could respond, he reached to unlatch her seatbelt, unlocked his door and stepped out, slamming it behind him. He came up to her door, opened it, took her hand, and pulled her out. "Come with me," he said.

"Where are we going?" she asked.

He frowned, pulling her along with him. "You locked your keys in the goddamned car," he said. "There's no way of getting them out without drawing suspicion and causing a scene." He growled. "I oughta spank your ass for that alone."

God, there he goes again, she thought, ignoring the pulsing between her legs and clenching of her belly and the hitch in her breathing. She should have been pissed at his threats.

His jaw clenched and his grip tightened as he brought her to a sedate looking two-story Cape-style house with a porch swing in the front, a white picket fence surrounding it, and vibrant orange marigolds in a small flower bed in the front yard. It looked so… *normal*.

He lived here?

"Get inside and don't say a word," he said, releasing her arm and unlocking the front door. He opened it, gestured for her to go in, and when she merely blinked at him, he swung his arm and smacked her ass, hard. "*Now.*"

Afraid he'd make good on his threat right here on the front porch, she trotted inside, her head swimming with anger, her body teeming with arousal… the way she always felt when in the presence of Diego Santiago.

Chapter 3

Diego slammed the solid wood door behind him and took grim satisfaction in the way Nora jumped at the sound, spun around, and huddled against the staircase bannister across from the front door. His heart was still beating rapidly and fury was gnawing a hole in his gut. *What had the woman been thinking, approaching the warehouse? Putting herself in danger like that?*

"Oh, *now* you're jumpy?" he demanded. "Well, thank fuck for that. I'd thought maybe you'd locked your fucking common sense in the car along with your keys."

Nora sniffed and clasped her hands at her waist. "I'm not jumpy. And I have plenty of common sense." Her voice quavered at the end, showing that she recognized the first half of her statement, at least, as a lie.

"Yeah? The same common sense that led you to a warehouse by the wharf in one of the roughest areas of Boston? To a warehouse that *you knew* was the headquarters of Chalo Salazar's enterprise? I can't *imagine* what other great ideas you might come up with. You need a fucking keeper."

He threw his keys into a small bowl on the hall table and

leaned back against the front door, crossing his arms over his chest as he watched her reaction. The motion made his bruised knuckles ache, but the pain hardly registered, he was so focused on the woman in front of him.

He'd be lying if he said he didn't appreciate the way she squirmed beneath his gaze, her tongue darting out to moisten her lips while her eyes darted from his biceps to his boots and back again. She was nearly shivering in the cool air, her thin sweater and skirt doing little to combat the chill inside the house, and he inhaled deeply at the sight, smelling the faint tang of the lemon polish that the house cleaners always used.

What the hell was he going to do with this woman?

That thought was quickly followed by another, even more troubling: *Why had he brought her* here *of all places, to the house that had been his mother's?* In truth, he wasn't behaving any more responsibly than Nora was tonight.

He couldn't think of anyone who even knew this house belonged to him, except maybe Slay, given that the annoying bastard knew everything. Though Diego kept the utilities on and the furniture just as it had been before his *Mamá* passed away, this was not the place where he crashed every night. He had a small efficiency apartment by the warehouse that suited that purpose. Instead, this house was his refuge, a place to commune with his ghosts and remember a time when the lines between good and evil, right and wrong, had been crystal clear. It was a place he came *alone*, on the rare occasions he visited, and he hadn't come at all for months. Yet, when he'd realized he needed to get Nora to safety tonight, it had been instinctive for him to bring her here. And even now, with anger and frustration still riding him, he couldn't deny that seeing her here, in *his* house, soothed something primal inside him.

"You have two seconds to explain exactly what the hell you hoped to learn at the warehouse tonight. And while you're at it,

I'd also like your sincere promise that you will *never even contemplate* stepping back into that neighborhood."

She looked at him warily and didn't speak, but his pulse kicked up as though she'd thrown down a gauntlet.

"No response, *Norita*?" he said. His voice was gruff as he challenged her. "Just gonna stand there?"

Her lips pursed, and her eyes narrowed. "I was afraid to speak, lest you decide to… to make good on your threat."

He felt his mouth twitch. "My threat?"

"To… to spank my ass," she spat, standing up straight and raising her chin defiantly. "Like a Neanderthal."

"Oh, sweetheart." He shook his head in mock sadness and continued in a silky voice, "That wasn't a *threat*. That was a *promise*." Her eyes widened with a combination of lust and anger, and his cock twitched. "Now answer my fucking questions."

She swallowed. "I already told you why I was there. I want answers."

"Because a little girl drew a picture of me," he said, repeating her words from earlier and injecting a heavy note of skepticism. "Some kid draws a smiley face or whatever, and you say 'Well, shit! That face has two eyes and a nose, just like Diego! Let me trot on down to the fucking warehouse, since clearly he keeps tabs on every kid in Boston! That's the smart, responsible choice.'"

"No! The girl—Camila—she's crazy talented. This was a picture of *you*. I-I know it." She stared at him defiantly, as though she expected him to deny it again and was ready to argue her case all night. He was shocked to find that his cock swelled behind the zipper of his jeans. *Christ.* What was it about this woman?

He took a step forward across the small space, crowding her against the bannister again, consciously intimidating her, since clearly she wasn't understanding his point. She smelled like grapefruit, and he willed himself not to notice how delicious the scent was. "I thought you said she drew a picture of someone who made her feel safe."

Nora nodded, and he smirked. "And am I the kind of man who makes you feel safe, baby?"

He almost laughed at the shock on her face, at the "no" that clearly wanted to spring to her lips. But at the last moment, he realized he didn't want to hear the denial. He was a dangerous man, and he was glad she recognized that, but he never wanted her to think he was a danger to *her*. "So how about you just promise me that you'll drop this bullshit, and stay the fuck away from that warehouse?"

She sucked in a breath, and he waited for her agreement. *Then you'll take her home*, he vowed to himself. *Where she's safe. And you'll call Slay and explain this epic clusterfuck and get him to make sure she keeps her promise.*

But when she glanced up at him, her eyes sparked with the intelligence and challenge that drove him crazy. "No."

Diego grit his teeth to keep his mouth from falling open. *Was she playing with him? Did she have no sense of self-preservation?*

He lifted one hand and wrapped his fingers loosely around the base of her throat. It was a move of blatant ownership and power, designed to make her tremble and rethink her hasty response, but the tremor that rocked her as his rough fingers stroked her skin wasn't one of fear, but anticipation and… *Jesus.* Arousal. And *that* look was what had him spinning her around with his hand on her hip until her fingers were gripping the stair rail. That look was what had him bending down to whisper in her ear, "Did you think I was joking, *mamita*?"

She shook her head minutely.

"Good. I fucking hope not. Because if there is one thing I have always taken seriously, it is your safety. Do you understand me?"

She was panting, and her hands spread out against the smooth wood, but she didn't answer. He reared back his hand

and then brought the palm of his uninjured hand down flat against her skirt-covered ass.

"Oh!" she gasped, a sound of surprise rather than pain.

He had to fight to keep the lust that clogged his throat from sounding in his voice when he growled, "No more questions. No more sticking your nose where it doesn't belong. Do you understand? It's not safe."

She glanced over her shoulder at him, her big brown eyes closer to his own than they'd been in years—or maybe ever. "I'm *not* dropping it. And you… you can't *bully* me into dropping it. I have a responsibility to the women at *Centered*, a responsibility to Camila, and…"

He cut her off with another firm smack to her ass. "I don't give a shit about what you think your responsibilities are! You need to keep yourself *safe*. You have no idea what you're dealing with. And I swear to you, I'm not letting you go until you get this."

"You're going to, what? Hold me hostage? Spank me into agreeing?" she demanded breathlessly. And the way her voice hitched told him that she was not nearly as averse to this idea as she should be. *Fuck.*

Was he going to go through with this? Though it had started as a threat to gain her compliance, one look at the defiant, hopeful spark in her eyes made the decision surprisingly easy, and his internal vow to let her go evaporated like mist. *Hell yes*, he was.

He grabbed her long hair and wrapped it tightly around his injured hand, forcing her to stand straight. "If that's what I have to do? Then, yes. You need some sense spanked into you. Someone should have done this a long time ago, *mamita.*"

He pulled her away from the wall with his hand in her hair, not harshly, but firmly, and forced her to walk ahead of him into the cozy living room to the left of the door. "Fortunately," he whispered, as he guided her towards the big leather sofa, "I'm more than up to the task."

He sat on the edge of the sofa and grabbed both of her hands, forcing her off-balance so that she landed over his lap gracelessly with a loud squawk.

"I'm not agreeing to anything!" she declared, as he tucked both of her hands firmly at the base of her spine and held them there. "You have no right to spank me. You're not my dominant, you're not my daddy, you're…"

He stopped her squirming with another firm swat to her ass from his uninjured hand, but he couldn't help but notice the way her skirt had ridden up as she struggled, giving him a clear view of her silky blue panties. He took a deep breath as a bolt of lust speared through him, and he delivered three more stinging swats in quick succession.

Those swats seemed to subdue her, to make her aware of the precariousness of her position for the first time. "Let me go, Diego!" she insisted. "This isn't funny anymore!"

"Funny? Fuck, honey. This hasn't been funny from the first minute that you rolled into my neighborhood. You came *alone*, into the most dangerous neighborhood in Boston, to demand answers from a *criminal*, and *locked your keys in your car*. You don't have the sense you were born with, and you're lucky this is the worst that happened! You *need* a daddy to protect you."

He spanked her again through the silk of her panties, peppering her ass and the tops of her thighs with firm blows. The skin of his palm was tingling, and even in the low light spilling from the entryway, he could see that the flesh on the top of her thighs was turning pink.

"You could have been killed. If anyone had seen you, you *would have been*. The men in my crew don't take too kindly to nosy girls." He spanked her again, struggling to keep control of his temper as the possibilities that might have befallen her raced through his mind.

"If any of my men had turned around? If I hadn't been making rounds of the warehouse *myself*, but had asked somebody *else* to do it? They would have caught you before I could save you, and do you know what would have happened?" *He* knew. He knew that if Ricky or any of the others had seen her, they'd never have kept their hands off her. And then Diego wouldn't have hesitated to kill him, to kill them *all*.

"Stop!" she demanded. "Diego! For fuck's sake stop!" But he wouldn't. Not until she understood.

"I'm *not* Diego right now, baby. I'm *not* the guy you demand answers from, and whose motives you question. Right now, in this room, I'm your keeper. I'm your goddamn *daddy*. So you'd better be a good little girl and get what I'm telling you right now —understand it in every part of you. You will *not* endanger yourself on my watch!"

Slap after slap, painful enough to sting but not to really hurt her, landed on her round ass as she writhed against him, and despite the fear that clutched at him, his dick was painfully hard and an insidious voice inside his head told him that the only way to save her, to protect her, was to claim her as his own. *Be her daddy. Make her your girl.*

His hand came to rest against the upper part of her ass, feeling the warmth of her reddened flesh through the thin material of her skirt as he kneaded her soft curves. "Do you trust me to keep you safe, baby? Tell Daddy."

She leaned against his leg, gasping for breath, and didn't answer right away. For a moment, he doubted himself. Maybe bringing her here had been the worst possible choice. If she *wouldn't* trust him, she'd never believe that this punishment had been aimed at forcing her to recognize the seriousness of her actions, and she'd only become more stubborn.

But a moment later, her gasps turned to quiet sobs, and she croaked, "Yes. Yes, I do. I don't know why, but I trust you… *Daddy.*"

Diego sucked in a breath and shut his eyes against the rush of pleasure that swamped him. *Daddy*. God, that was so not his kink... or at least it never had been. But now, hearing it from her? He didn't know how he'd gone so long without it.

He didn't deserve her trust—if the woman only knew half the things he'd said and done over the years, she'd run screaming. And he knew that what little she *did* know had always made her question his motives. But there was a ring of truth in her voice that he couldn't deny. She trusted him here and now. And since she did, maybe he wasn't an entirely lost cause after all.

Wetness against his leg had him releasing her hands and hauling her up to sit across his lap with her head against his chest.

"Hush, baby," he said, running his hands down her hair and over her light sweater. "Hush, my good girl."

But she only sobbed harder, like a dam somewhere inside her had broken, and buried her face against his neck.

"I-I'm sorry," she whispered. "I was impulsive and stupid. The minute I got there, I realized I was totally in over my head, but then you were there and I... I couldn't admit it," she hiccupped softly.

He understood that feeling only too well, but he needed to make sure nothing like this ever happened again. Not to her. "Your first priority, Nora, in every single thing you do, every single day, must be your own safety. You're devoted to your job, to your family, to your friends, and so many people love you and want to keep you safe. But ultimately, the only person who can do that is *you*, understand?"

Her chin bumped his shoulder as she nodded, but her tears didn't abate. He grasped her neck and pulled her back slightly, reaching over to flick on the nearby lamp so he could see her face.

He carefully brushed her tangled, damp hair away from her

flushed cheeks. "It's all done now, honey. You took your spanking like such a good girl. I'm so proud of you."

Her sobs mingled with laughter. "God, why does that sound so good?" she wondered with a groan. "I swear, I always thought the daddy thing was a little odd, but when you talk to me like that… it does something to my belly. Like I want to be all vulnerable and let you protect me."

His breath caught at the confusion and trust that mingled in her wide eyes. "I want to protect you. That's all I've *ever* wanted to do," he told her, carding his fingers through her hair and inhaling the citrusy fragrance.

"I believe you," she said simply. And then she shocked the shit out of him by leaning forward and touching her lips gently to his.

Madre de Dios, had anything ever felt so good? Her lips were soft and cool against his, cleansing and nourishing him, and without conscious decision, he opened his mouth beneath hers, wanting to draw her closer. He'd given up hope years ago that this would ever happen, but as he gripped her blonde hair and tasted the salt of her tears in her kiss, he recognized that it had been inevitable.

His free hand wrapped around her back, pulling her chest more firmly against his, and she twisted until she could bring one leg over his lap to straddle him. Her skirt rode up all the way to her hips as she settled her sweet ass directly above the erection that was trying to poke its way out of his jeans. *Fuck.*

Mine, his brain chanted on constant repeat. *Finally mine.*

His hand coasted up her side and his thumb teased the underside of her breast. He swallowed her gasp and felt her nipple bead as he stroked her lightly. His lips broke from hers and moved to explore her jaw, alternately licking and sucking against her neck as she writhed against him, torturing them both.

He grabbed the bottom of her sweater and pulled it up and over her head in one smooth movement, throwing it somewhere behind the couch. He disposed of her lacy bra in exactly the same fashion, hardly noticing the sexiness of the garment in his quest to bare her—all of her, every inch of her luscious skin—to his gaze. He flipped them so her back was against the seat cushions, then knelt beside her, pulling her skirt and panties down with the same hurried determination.

But when she was splayed out naked before him, time seemed to stop, and he sat back on his heels, staring at the vision before him. *God, she was beautiful.*

She was pale and perfect, from her rosy-tipped breasts to the small patch of blonde hair above her pussy. He could feel her eyes on his as his gaze tracked a path from her shapely legs, over the curve of her hips and belly, to her face. She bit her lip and moved her hand to cover herself, but he stopped her with a firm grip on her wrist. There was not a single thing about her that wasn't stunning, and he knew his voice was nearly drunk with desire when he whispered, "You're perfect, baby. Let me look at you." *Let me figure out which part of you to worship first.*

He couldn't keep himself from bending forward and capturing one taut nipple between his lips, then tormenting the stiff flesh with his tongue while his fingers sought her other nipple. Despite the hunger he'd felt for her all these years, he'd never allowed himself to fantasize about this happening. He'd never allowed himself to imagine what she'd look like splayed out before him, how sweet she would taste, or how her breathless moans and gasps would drive him wild.

With his free hand, he fumbled for his zipper, and his erection sprang free.

"Oh my God. You don't wear underwear," she whispered inanely, glancing downward, then giggled at her own observation. "I don't know what I expected, I mean, badass that you are and all, but… *Holy shit.*"

He snickered as his teeth clamped gently around her sensitive flesh, but then it was his turn to hiss out a breath as her hand snaked into the opening of his pants and gripped him tightly.

"You're playing with fire again, little girl," he warned her, his voice rough as sandpaper.

But her eyes met his with that determined spark that never failed to light him up. "I think I can handle this, Daddy," she whispered, and his dick literally throbbed.

He braced his knee on the couch and leaned over her, trailing his hand down her stomach to toy with her curls. "Let's see about that, baby."

God in heaven, her pussy was completely drenched, and Diego felt his mind short-circuit for half a moment with the knowledge that she—*his Nora*—was every bit as turned on by this as he was. He stroked her folds carefully, loving the way her hips rose to meet his, and his eyes rolled back in his head as her hand stroked him in the same rhythm.

"More, Daddy," she begged, releasing his cock so that she could tug impatiently at his jeans. "I want you in me... *now*."

He hurried to comply, shucking his heavy boots, as well as his t-shirt and jeans. He resumed his place above her, his fingers playing with her core while his mouth claimed hers in a brutal clash of teeth and tongues. But when she reached up to try to pull his body down to her, he shook his head.

"I don't have a condom, Nora." He'd long ago stopped carrying them, knowing that the fucking things expired and he wasn't planning to use one. "And you left your purse in your car."

"I don't *care*," she cried, writhing against his hand. "Please, Daddy. I want you inside me so badly."

Fuck. His eyes squeezed shut and his breath caught, more aroused than he'd ever been in his life. His urge to claim her, to please her, to own her, was a fire in his chest, but even then, his need to protect her overrode all else.

"Not today, little one," he told her firmly. "Not without

protection. Not without discussing it first. But Daddy's going to take care of you. You'll see."

He plunged two fingers inside her and she bucked off the sofa, whimpering softly. He slid down the couch and braced his forearm over her pelvis, holding her in place, while he laved her warm pussy with his tongue until her head flew back and she came apart for him.

He continued to work her gently with his tongue, riding out her orgasm, but the moment her tremors stopped, he lifted himself up in one smooth movement and rose to straddle her.

"Fuck you're sweet, baby. Sweetest pussy I've ever tasted. Was that good? Hmm? Tell me, little girl."

She moaned beneath him, her lip caught between her teeth and her eyes still hazy with lust. "Do you want me to…" she began, but he cut her off and his own hand moved towards his cock, jacking slowly.

"All I want you to do is lay right there. Fuck. Lay right there in front of me, so Daddy can see that beautiful face, those gorgeous breasts."

His left hand moved up to squeeze her sensitized nipple, and her pained gasp made his balls draw up tight. He moved his hand faster and faster, loving the way her eyes were glued to his cock as he worked himself.

"Who owns this?" he demanded, squeezing again roughly. "Who does this belong to now?"

Her own breath was coming in pants, as understanding of what was about to happen dawned in her eyes. "To you, Daddy," she whimpered, bracing her hands on his thighs. "You own it."

"Fucking right, I do," he told her, and then he exploded, rope after rope of cum shooting all over her chest, marking her. *Branding her*.

He leaned over her, wrecked with the force of his orgasm, and braced himself on one hand while with the other, he trailed a finger through the mess on her chest, smearing it over her breasts, rubbing it into her nipples. Her eyes watched his finger as it circled, and he felt her belly quiver.

"Mine," he growled. It wasn't a question. It was a command. It was a statement of fact as unquestionable in that moment as the pull of gravity.

And when her eyes lifted to meet his, they were soft and fathomless, with not a hint of a challenge.

"Yours, Daddy," she agreed, and she lifted her head to seal her promise with a kiss.

"PADRE. I expected to hear from you yesterday," the voice on the other end of the phone reproved. Diego sank into the oversized arm chair in the living room, the well-worn leather barely squeaking as he shifted.

"I apologize, Jefe," Diego replied, barely keeping the impatience out of his voice. "Many things came up yesterday that required my attention."

"Hmmm," the voice said, and whatever voice-altering equipment the bastard known as El Jefe used made the humming noise not only disbelieving, but downright sinister. "So I heard."

A tremor of unease skittered up Diego's spine. "What have you heard?"

El Jefe had spies all over the city—hell, all up and down the Eastern seaboard, so it wasn't a surprise to know that the asshole had spies within Diego's crew, as well. It had only been a matter of time before he learned that the girl—*Camila*, had escaped from the warehouse.

To be perfectly honest, Diego hadn't given much thought to what would happen to Camila after he dropped her at *Centered*. He'd figured that Nora, Elena, and Alice would get the girl the help she needed, and that Slay and his crew would make sure Camila stayed safe. But now, thinking about the woman he'd left sleeping safe and warm in his bed upstairs, those assumptions no longer seemed like enough. He couldn't help but wonder if his rash actions yesterday morning—and again last night—would bring trouble to Nora's door, and he'd be damned if he'd let his shit touch her.

She was his to protect, now more than ever.

El Jefe laughed, high and sinister. "That's not how this works, Padre. When I contact you, you give *me* information, not the other way around."

As the rising sun turned the sky outside pink and orange, Diego ran his tongue over his teeth and pondered the best response—the one least likely to get anyone, including himself, killed.

"The man who was on guard duty last night made an error in judgment and entered the cell where the girl was being held. He's not sure how it happened, but somehow she managed to knock him out and locked him in the cell as she escaped. He woke up a little while later, but he didn't have his phone on him, so no one knew what had happened until yesterday morning when the rest of the guys showed up."

Diego paused, but El Jefe remained silent, so he continued. "I made sure that he was punished."

His heart beat quickly, waiting for El Jefe to ask about the details of the punishment. If Tomás, or anyone else who'd felt like Diego hadn't punished Ricky severely enough, was El Jefe's informant, Diego was certain that El Jefe would ask, and possibly demand proof that Ricky had been terminated by Diego's own hand. His stomach churned at the thought.

But El Jefe turned the conversation in a different direction. "And the girl? What steps have you taken to recover her?"

"Recover her?" Diego repeated. "How? There were no clues as to where the girl had gone. No cars were missing, so she obviously fled on foot. And you know we don't allow any type of cameras anywhere near the warehouse, so there's no security footage." This was an unusual rule instituted during Salazar's reign that Diego found to be both a blessing and a curse. It meant he didn't have any photographic evidence of the shit that went down there, but it also meant that his face was not well-known in criminal circles, nor even by El Jefe himself. "I felt that making inquiries about her would raise too many red flags." In fact, he'd been nearly certain that El Jefe would praise his forethought. Apparently he'd been wrong.

"Did you?" El Jefe asked. "Interesting."

Diego fought the urge to defend himself, knowing it would only be a sign of guilt.

"It wasn't because this girl was a bit younger than the other girls we've dealt with?" El Jefe continued. "You wouldn't have grown a conscience at this late date, would you, Padre? Knowing that the girl would have to be killed to prevent her from speaking to the authorities, let alone testifying against any of you?"

"No," Diego said shortly. "I would do what had to be done, as I always have. I'd take no pleasure in it, though," he added bitterly, hoping that this small amount of truth would help sell the lie.

It appeared to work. "That's good," El Jefe said. "Very good. That's why you're indispensable as my lieutenant, Padre. I know I can count on you to take care of your end of the business, while I deal with the complications on my end."

"And what complications would those be?" Diego asked, rolling his eyes because he knew that after all this time working for the organization, after all the hours that Slay's crew had spent backing through Salazar's twisted financial records, looking for clues about the source of his payments, there was no way someone as private as El Jefe would provide Diego with a single detail about his operation.

Unsurprisingly, El Jefe laughed. "That's for me to know, Padre. But back to the girl. It turns out I *do* have some information for you. She turned up at a shelter called *Centered*," he said, and Diego could swear his heart skipped a beat. "She's underage, so she's not living on-site, but she'll be there for counseling for the next few days at least."

"*Centered*," Diego repeated, forcing his voice to stay level. "I think I've heard of it."

"Mmm. It was in the news not long ago. Ironically, it's run by the wife of that man Chalo Salazar hated so much. Blaine?"

"Blake," Diego said hoarsely, knowing that El Jefe was just testing him. "His name is Blake."

"Ah, yes," El Jefe agreed. "Runs that club that Marauder had such a hard-on for. Blake called too much attention to Chalo's organization. He dragged Chalo's name through the mud before the poor bastard met his maker!" The robotic voice was almost gleeful, but then turned serious. "But that was because Chalo Salazar left far too many loose ends. That won't happen to us, Padre. Now that you know the girl's whereabouts, I trust I can count on you to take care of the situation."

Fuck, fuck, fuck.

"It won't be easy, *Jefe*," Diego stalled. "If you know that Blake is involved, you have to know that the same security team that guards his club also guards *Centered*. Trying to get in there to snatch the girl would be suicide and call unwanted attention to us, just as it did to Salazar…"

"Don't be an idiot," El Jefe said, his voice hard and cold even through the scrambler. "You won't touch a hair on the girl's head at *Centered*. But you *will* investigate the place. Find out where they have her staying and grab her there. Or while she's in transit, when her security is weakest. You know how this works, Padre. I'm not going to do your job for you."

"No, *Jefe*," Diego said. "I understand."

"Good. And understand this," El Jefe continued. "I want this situation resolved by next Saturday. *One. Week.* No more. Or else I might not find you so indispensable in the future."

The phone made an audible click, like it was being disconnected, but Diego sat motionless with the phone still held to his ear for a minute longer.

Goddamn it. He'd need to call Slay and work out a plan for dealing with this, although nothing immediately sprang to mind. He had one week to figure out a way to bring down the organization—a feat he hadn't been able to accomplish in *years*—or Slay and his contacts would pull him from the investigation whether he wanted to be or not. And since sticking around would mean letting El Jefe oust Diego from his position—not simply by beating the shit out of him as he'd done to Ricky, but with torture and double-tap to the head—Diego was definitely not going to fight Slay over being pulled.

He was surprised, a moment later, to find that his mind had never, even for a second, considered actually harming Camila in order to maintain his cover. Just yesterday, he'd been wondering where his ultimate loyalty lay and whether there was anything he wouldn't do to complete this investigation. Today, it appeared he'd gotten his answer: Nora. Anything that would hurt *her*, that would prevent his woman from trusting him fully, was officially off the table.

Just as he went to lower the phone, he heard a scrabbling sound on the other end of the line, and he realized the call was still connected. He pulled the phone away from his ear and found that the timer was still counting. The call was still engaged.

Sounding like it was coming from a great distance, he heard the slam of a door, followed by the scrape of a chair. And then a voice, much higher than the deep bass tone of the voice changer, but with the unmistakable cadence of El Jefe's, said, "Don't lie to me, Miguel!" There was a slapping sound, and then…

"Who are you talking to, Daddy?"

Nora's shy, sleepy voice greeted him from the entryway of the room, and Diego's eyes flew to her. She looked so hesitant standing there, as if uncertain now that so much had changed between them.

Without a second's pause, he disconnected the call. No way in hell did he want El Jefe to realize that the line was still open, nor give the bastard a chance to hear Nora's voice at the other end. He shut his eyes and blew out a breath at the opportunity he'd just missed at listening in on El Jefe. Then he opened them, to find Nora approaching him with a small smile on her face.

"Diego?" she repeated shyly. "I mean… Daddy?"

He sucked in a breath and held out his arm in unspoken invitation, and she happily sat on his lap.

"I like my shirt on you," he told her, running his hands down the faded Red Sox t-shirt that covered her back and loving the way she burrowed against his chest.

"It smells like you," she said, her voice muffled against his sweatshirt. "Like wood smoke and the cologne you wore years ago when you… when you rescued me."

He switched his grip to run his hand down the warmth of her bare leg, and took a moment to appreciate the fact that he *could*. That she was here, in his home, in his arms, when he'd never expected her to be. "And now it'll smell like you," he said gruffly. "Like grapefruit and vanilla."

"It's my shampoo," she said, and he smiled.

"I'll have to buy that shit in bulk, then. Because I'm pretty sure after last night, that smell alone is gonna get me off. I haven't come that hard in years."

She leaned back and her eyes flew to his face, while a pretty blush stained her cheeks. "Years?"

"Years," he confirmed, and her teeth gnawed at her bottom lip. "Why?"

"Because it's been years for me, too," she told him. As he watched, the fire came back into her eyes, and he had to fight a groan as his body responded. They didn't have time for another round right now, and the next time he took her, he was going to have fucking protection.

He was about to tell her that he needed to call Slay, and that there was coffee in the kitchen—though that was pretty much the *only* thing in the kitchen, given how infrequently he came to this place—when she spoke again, haltingly.

"So what happens now?" she asked. "You're still… undercover?"

He pulled her into his chest again and nodded against the top of her head. "*Si, mamita.* Still undercover. But… possibly not for long."

She leaned back to look at him. "Really? What changed? Yesterday you were still committed, and…"

He shook his head. Even if he wanted to be honest with her about some part of his life or his undercover work, he couldn't be. Keeping her ignorant meant keeping her safe.

"Doesn't matter, baby," he said instead. But when she scowled at his evasion, he conceded, "I'll tell you what I can, when I can." It wouldn't be much, though. He had far too many things he never wanted her to know about him. "Tell me about you. Tell me about your friends. And *Centered*."

She nodded, though her narrowed eyes told him that she would hold him to his agreement and wouldn't let him evade her questions for long. She filled him in on her job, and the various services they provided at *Centered*. How it had grown from a neighborhood women's medical clinic to also become a shelter and resource center for both women and children. She talked about the women she'd helped, and the resources she provided them. She very carefully avoided mention of Camila, of the picture the girl had drawn and all the questions that had led Nora to him the night before, but he knew she'd demand answers to those questions, in particular, very soon. And she talked about the incredible women she worked with—women who'd become her friends and mentors over the years.

"Oh, and I'm heading a fundraiser," she told him with a laugh. "I'm a little nervous, but Diana Consuelos—she's one of our main donors—she tells me I need to keep challenging myself if I want to reach my potential. I had this idea where, instead of our usual black-tie fundraisers, we'd do a field day for the kids and parents alike. We'll have a band, and face painting, and those beanbag-toss booths where you can win prizes."

"That sounds great, baby," he said, loving her enthusiasm.

She nodded happily. "The last couple of fundraisers, Elena organized by herself, and they were black-tie deals. We wore gowns donated from this pricey Newbury Street boutique. It was fun, but…well, *fancy*. Not my kinda thing."

"You don't dig the Cinderella vibe?" he teased.

"Well, the dress didn't leave much room for the imagination, but beggars can't be choosers," she told him, poking him playfully. "Hillary said I looked hot. Next time one of these black tie events comes up, you'll see what I mean." Her face grew troubled. "I-if you're around, I mean."

He looked at her sternly. "I will absolutely be around," he told her. "But you might wish I weren't, Norita, if you tell me you're going to dress in something I won't find appropriate."

Her mouth dropped open. "But… really? That's not fair," she argued. "You don't get to say—"

"Oh, baby, you don't get how this works," he informed her, his eyes trapping hers. "I'm your *daddy*." The words sent a thrill up his spine. "Therefore, I get a say in anything that impacts your health, safety, and well-being… *for a start*. We'll build from there. But in the meantime," he continued, settling her against him, when is this Field Day Fundraiser?"

She still seemed nonplussed by his earlier statements, and he almost chuckled. "Er, a week from tomorrow? It's at Memorial Field in Cambridge."

A week from tomorrow. He suddenly realized just how drastically different his life would look in another week and, since this was turning out to be a morning of revelations, he allowed himself to imagine a scenario where he could escort her to the damn fundraiser… to *all* her future fundraisers… and assault any man who dared to look at the curves her dress showed off.

"So, I guess I'll be spending the whole next week finalizing every single detail," Nora had continued, apparently not recognizing the direction of his thoughts. "But that's okay, because *Centered* is… well, it saved me, in a way. You know what it was like for me and Tess growing up. I mean, probably better than anyone." She gave him a wry smile.

Diego linked his fingers through hers. "You were always so strong, *mi vida*."

"Eh. I was snarky," she corrected with a smirk. "Snarky's not strong. Not always. This… us… what we did last night? I don't think I would have been able to do that a few years back. I was too scared of being dependent to give up control."

"And now you're not?" he laughed. "It's easy as pie for you?"

"Oh, no, I'm still scared to death," she admitted. "Scared of this, scared of us, scared of… you, being undercover, and whatever the fuck that means. I have no idea what I'm doing. But… but now I'm strong enough to *try*, I think."

"It's not something I have a lot of experience with, either, *Norita*," he admitted. "I've been to The Club, and the circle we run in is pretty open about the type of relationship they all have. But this? Having a girl of my own, being her daddy? It's new for me too. Trust me, baby. Trust *us*, and we'll make it work," he vowed, running his hand over her hair. And then he fell silent, taking in the quiet stillness of the morning that surrounded them, as a new purpose cemented itself in his mind. He'd protect her and this new thing that was growing between them, no matter the cost.

Chapter 4

Nora listened to Diego's low murmur on the phone in the other room. Frowning, she glanced at her phone. Three phone calls in the matter of five minutes? On a Sunday morning?

What exactly was she getting into with Diego Santiago?

Who was it that demanded his attention on the other end of the line? She was smart enough to know that Camila had fallen victim to Diego's crew, but to what extent? She could easily surmise a few things, though. First, whatever undercover shit he did involved young girls. Second, it was dangerous enough that he'd seen red when she came near the men he worked with. Third, Diego was in danger, and if she was going to be anywhere near him… she was, too.

Why didn't she feel afraid, then? Maybe it was because their imminent danger had a surreal quality about it, making it too hard to grasp the reality of their situation. Maybe it was because she'd realized that he *was* the good guy she'd always hoped he was, and not the scary asshole he pretended to be. Or maybe… maybe it was because she truly did trust him to protect her, to take care of her in whatever way necessary.

Her ass still stung from the punishing smack of his palm. God... he'd *spanked* her. She shifted on the chair at the kitchen table, squirming at the memory of being face-down over his lap, his strong grip holding her in place as he spanked her again and again...

Her heart thumped a crazy beat in her chest and she clenched her thighs together. She'd hated showering last night, washing evidence of his claiming off of her. God, that had been the sexiest fucking thing she'd ever done, and her mind replayed every delicious detail. Every other guy she'd been with had been a nice, proper gentleman who made her big sister Tessa proud. She'd dated good men who carried condoms in their wallets and played the rules: kiss first, up it to second base after dinner involving wine, fondle a bit after established trust, no sex until the time was right. They would tell her she was pretty, and buy her flowers, and then they'd have missionary sex with the lights off. Diego had done none of those things. He'd taken her across his knee in punishment, made her climax, then claimed her with his own pleasure.

She closed her eyes, cradling her head in her hands as she remembered the way Diego's eyes heated, fixed on hers, daring her to move as he came on her naked skin, the tortured way he'd finally given into ecstasy.

"Nora." His deep, commanding voice from the doorway made her jump. He smiled grimly. "Scared so easily, baby? You were deep in thought." He crossed the room and took her hand. "So small," he said, so softly it was almost as if to himself. "She places her hand in mine just like this." One hand went over the other, and both his hands engulfed hers as he brought her fingers to his lips and kissed them, the prickles of his whiskers contrasting with the warmth and tenderness of his mouth. Arousal pooled in her belly, desire threading through her limbs at the feel of his lips against her hand, her heart warming to his gentle touch.

She'd lost all control.

He lifted her to her feet, before circling his arm around her waist and drawing her closer to him. "Let's go, before I lose my mind and do something drastic." His mouth came to her ear, his low drawl making her shiver. "Like eat *you* for breakfast instead."

Aw, *fuck*. Her eyes fluttered closed as her knees wobbled.

"Stop teasing me," she muttered in a breathy protest. "I need you to… do something serious, and stop messing with my mind. I can't handle it."

Chuckling, he placed one hand on her jaw and tilted her face upward, his mouth meeting hers in a kiss that was at once strong, possessive, and heated. He held her against his warm, strong body as he kissed her, slowly, softly, then more intensely, a moan escaping from deep within her at the taste of his kiss before he pulled away and shook his head. "I need to go," he said hoarsely.

"Fuck no," she moaned, earning her a sharp slap to the ass. Her pussy pulsed, her breath hitched, and she swallowed against rising arousal.

"I don't like hearing those words come out of your pretty mouth," he said. "Little girls ought to watch their language."

She grinned against his chest. "Yeah, Daddy? So if I say *fuck* or *shit* or *motherfucking whore*, what are you gonna do about it?" In all the years she'd known him, they'd never been able to joke like this, to tease. He'd always held himself aloof and watched her from a distance, and she'd never admitted to herself just how deeply her feelings for him ran.

"You know what I'll do about it, you little brat," he whispered up against her ear. "I'll wash your mouth out with soap and send you to bed without dinner."

She laughed out loud as he teased her, his fingers threading through her hair and trailing along her scalp before resting on her neck. He pulled her against his chest, her body flush with his, and she felt his rock hard erection pressed against her belly. She swallowed. He enjoyed this game as much as she did.

"A soapy mouth is so *sexy*, Daddy," she said with a laugh, and he pulled her even closer.

His mouth up against her ear, his breath traveled along the back of her neck as he whispered. "No, baby. I'm just teasing you. I wouldn't punish you with childish consequences. I'd pull you over my knee, pull your panties to your ankles, and spank your bare ass." She moaned. "And if you pushed it, I'd take my belt to you."

Her thighs clenched and her heart stuttered as he continued. "Or maybe I'd bend you over the back of the couch and strip you," he said. "Then I'd whip your ass and teach you to mind your daddy."

Oh, fuck. She was gonna come if he kept this up. Her clit pulsed, her heart was stuttering in her chest, her breath coming in little gasps. He pushed his hand between her legs, a firm touch that instantly claimed what was his, raking up her skirt and threading along the silken strip of fabric between her legs.

"Is that what you want, Nora?" he whispered, fingering her over her panties. A moan escaped her lips as her forehead fell to his chest. "Are you a naughty little girl? Do you get off on imagining Daddy spanking you with his belt? Do you, baby?" The tempo of his strokes increased and she began to grind against his hand, willing him not to stop. "If I took off your panties, would I find you wet for me, baby? Hmm?"

Oh, God, oh please, she silently begged, needing to feel him, needing to find release against him. Slowly, his fingers gripped the edge of her panties and pushed them away before dipping lower.

"God, baby, you're soaked," he said with a dark chuckle. "So primed for me. That a girl," he said as his fingers stroked her clit expertly. She was going to come standing up against him in his kitchen. She buried her face against him as he fingered her, his words making her desire mount with every breath. "Good girl," he said. "That's it, baby. What a beautiful, naughty little girl you are. You ought to have your ass whipped and your pussy fucked every single goddamned day." He chuckled again. She was completely under his control, as he stroked her. She was going to lose control, right on the cusp when his voice dropped, commanding now. "Come on Daddy's fingers, baby."

And with that, she lost control, writhing against his hand as he stroked her to climax, her pulse racing, moaning low, her gasps unbidden with her face still buried in his chest as he braced her with one hand behind her back. Finally, he removed his fingers and pulled her up against his chest. "Does a man good to see a girl come like that," he said softly. She hid her face, enjoying his warmth and strength. He smelled so good, felt so strong.

"God, baby, I want you to sit on my face," he said, stroking his hands through her hair. "I'd love to spend all day doing wicked things to you until your voice was hoarse from screaming my name." She swallowed, needing him to stop and needing him to continue. "But I have to go now. You'll stay here, and I won't take too long."

Wait a minute.

"Um… Diego?" she said, pulling her head off his chest and looking up at his dark eyes that had grown more tender now, and not quite as guarded. He brushed a piece of hair off over her forehead and tucked it behind her ear.

"Yeah, baby?"

"I… I'm not going with you? I'm staying here? I don't want to stay here alone. I have things to do," she protested, hating the idea of him leaving her here like this. She had a job to do, damn it, people who were depending on her. And if she were honest, she hated the idea of his leaving her. The very idea left her bereft.

His lips thinned and his eyes shuttered again, losing the softer edge she'd seen just seconds before. He was no longer her daddy but Padre, the man who commanded the insidious ring of criminals. "Yeah, Nora," he said with a sigh, releasing her. "Slay's man is outside. He'll watch you while I attend to… business," he said, his eyes flitting away from hers as his voice faltered. He released her, and her heart sank to her toes.

"Oh," she said in a little voice. "God, Diego, if Slay's man is outside, does that mean Tess…"

If her sister knew she'd spent the night with Diego… if any of them knew… they'd have questions even she didn't have the answer to.

He shook his head. "Only Slay and his guy know you're here, honey. Nobody else even knows I own this place. And I'll be back within the hour. Today, I'm spending time with you. It's supposed to be my day off." He raked a hand through his hair, making it stand up on end. "But I have shit to take care of after the calls I made this morning. When I'm done, I'll pick you up and we'll get some food in town before I take you to work." He paused, and a glimmer of hope shone once again in his eyes. "It's been a long time since I've done normal things, Nora. I want that. I'm done with the lies and secrecy I've had to wallow in, and I can't wait until we can put all that behind us and move on. But today? I want you to tell me what's going on with you. We'll talk, and eat, and get to know each other a bit more." His lips quirked at the edges and he once again tucked a stray piece of hair behind her ear. "Yeah?"

She reached out to touch his hand, sliding her palm against his. "Yeah," she whispered, wanting to heal him of the torture that lingered in his eyes. Deep down in her very soul she wanted to make him happy, so she did the one thing she knew that would make him smile. She'd give that to him. Holding his hand against hers, she whispered, "I'd like that, Daddy."

He blinked, then grinned, pulled her over to him and gave her a final parting kiss before pulling away. "Okay, honey." He let her go and took her hand, leading her into the living room. "Let's get you situated."

As she nestled back on the sofa, her gaze wandered about the room. The windows were simply dressed with light green curtains that fluttered in the breeze. October in New England occasionally welcomed warm weather. Though the evenings frequently brought the chilly air, today was pleasantly warm. To the left of the curtains, a fireplace flanked one wall, directly across from where they sat on the sofa. Along the mantle sat framed prints, five in all. She squinted, trying to see them, as he rummaged around, getting his phone and wallet.

"Who are all those people on the mantle?" she asked.

"Those are pictures of my family," he said. "I have three brothers and a sister."

"Wow. Your mama had five kids?" she asked, but he shook his head.

"No. She had six, baby. But my other brother, Armando, died when we were teenagers." A chill came over her, and her heart twisted in her chest.

"God. That's terrible." Her voice broke and a lump rose in her throat. She wanted to cry for Diego, for his mama who'd had to bury her child. But she would stay strong for him.

"No more talk of this, Nora. I need to go. I'll take care of moving your car and bring you your things later, but in the meantime you do not leave here."

She wanted to ask more. She wanted to know what made him tick, what he needed to see happen with his investigation, what had happened to his brother, but the tone of his voice brooked no argument. "I'll be back. You stay here and entertain yourself. There's TV, and you can use my old laptop. Surf the web or whatever, but under no circumstances do you tell anyone where you are." His gaze sobered as he lifted a finger and pointed it at her. "Do you understand me?" And just like that, her mind had her over his knee as he spanked her.

"Yes, Daddy," she said. He grinned. And then he was gone.

NORA TAPPED her foot while she surfed the web on his laptop. She paid a few bills, and then checked her email, tossing out junk mail, and sifting through until she found a few from work. The top one from Gretchen Liu, an investigative reporter who was close friends with Elena, concerned her.

"Hey, Nora. Can you send me the contact info for those women *Centered* helped last year? Alice sent it to me last week, but I think something's wrong. I tried to contact a few of them, and it seems that all of their numbers have either changed or they weren't right. I haven't been able to get in touch with a single one of them."

Nora frowned. As part of the big fundraiser *Centered* was planning, they'd hoped to have some testimonies from former clients, those who were willing to speak of the changes they'd made since coming to *Centered*. *Centered* had helped countless women get on their feet after tragedy or struggles, thanks in no small part to the generosity of *Centered's* largest benefactor, Diana Conseulos, who'd become a sort of mentor to Nora. Diana herself had helped their recent clients relocate to Miami and get new jobs. It was not uncommon for clients to move, and they didn't often stay in touch, but some did. It was weird that Gretchen couldn't get in touch with any of these women. Nora responded to the email and promised Gretchen she'd get back to her soon, then stood up and stretched.

She walked over to the window and pulled the edge of the filmy light green curtain back. There, right below her window, sat the large black car with the shadow of a driver in it: Slay's guy, the one Diego had likely called twelve times since he'd left.

She hadn't disobeyed him. She was right where she said she'd be.

But when he came back, she'd maybe push that envelope.

What had he said about taking his belt to her? *God.* She

leaned back against the couch and closed her eyes, fingers traveling under the edge of her skirt, between her legs to tease her clit. She bit her lip and stroked herself, imagining Diego coming into the house, his dark eyes furious. Somehow, it was hotter when he was pissed off. He'd never lose control with her. This she knew. But that look he got when he was angry…

She closed her eyes and snuggled down on his sofa, imagining him coming into the room, his dark brown eyes furious, that look that he gave somewhere between passion and fury. He'd come into the room, storm up to her, and grab her with those powerful hands of his. She'd struggle, but he was so much stronger. He'd pull her bodily over his knee, and then—

The door to the house opened and her hands flew out of her panties, smoothing down her skirt, as she heard the door slam. She looked around her, her heart thumping madly in her chest. Was it Diego? Who else would walk in the house and slam the door?

"Norita," came Diego's low voice, thickened with his Spanish accent. "What are you doing?" She folded her hands on her lap, attempting to do her very best to plaster a look of innocence on her face.

"Oh, nothing," she said.

He sat on the arm of the couch, folding his arms across his chest as his eyes narrowed on hers. "Really?" he said. "Then why do you look so guilty? Were you reading? Surfing the web?"

She sat up straighter and smoothed out the nonexistent wrinkles in her skirt. "Um. Well, I checked my email and that was fine, and then I… sat on the couch and I… um…" God, she sucked at lying. She cleared her throat and looked at him from beneath lowered lashes. What did she have to lose? "I… maybe… was… um…"

He pushed off the arm of the couch and plunked down on the seat next to her. She glanced at the breadth of his lap, and wondered briefly what it *would* be like if she were over his lap again. Would it feel nice to sit on his lap and put her head on his shoulder? To lay her head on his chest and just *relax* for once? But he sat apart from her, eying her with a wary glance.

"What were you doing, Nora?" he asked, his voice deepening now, as he grew more serious. "And why are you acting as if there's something you need to tell me?"

She felt her lips pulling down in a frown. Gone was the sweet man who'd taken her to climax just that morning before he'd left, the man she'd called *daddy*, and in his place sat the aloof leader of a ring of criminals. It was just like that night in the warehouse. How could he turn his warmth on and off like that? How could she trust anything he told her?

What the fuck was she doing?

"Something to tell you?" she asked, getting to her feet as she turned away and shook her head. She'd made a horrible, horrible mistake. "No, I've nothing to tell you. I'm all set, thanks," she said. "In fact, honestly, Diego, it's really time I go. Slay's guy outside will drive me. I'll get something to eat on the way to work." Her voice shook a bit. God, she was with a criminal, a man who *supposedly* was merely an undercover agent. But how much did she *really* know about him? She needed to get the hell out of here. She turned to go when his low, angry voice arrested her.

"Don't you *dare*."

Slowly, she turned around, her pulse increasing at the chiding tone he used. When she faced him, he sat with his arms crossed on his chest, his stubbled jaw tightened. "Get your ass over here," he ordered.

Her fists clenched at her sides as she drew in breath. "And if I say no?" she whispered. "What then, *Daddy?*" She threw the word back at him, wanting to hurt him, wanting to make him feel the pain she did. "Will you *spank* me?"

He only continued to stare, his eyes burning a hole in her. A muscle twitched in his jaw before he replied. "Yes."

No discussion, explanation, or threats. No. He meant it. He expected her to walk over to him and if she didn't, he'd spank her. As her mind reeled with her choices, she asked herself what she was playing at. Why had she allowed him to rile her so badly? What had caused her to be so pissed off with him? Had she allowed herself to be fooled?

No. She'd allowed herself to become vulnerable.

And now she was scared.

Though she wanted this, was it *real?* Was it *true?*

The deep sound of his voice made her start. "You have ten seconds, Nora."

Her eyes flitted to the doorway. Ten seconds! If she made a run for it now, she could make it, maybe, if he didn't pursue her. If he tried to grab her, she could beat him off, but getting into a physical skirmish with a guy twice her size was just plain stupid. She could stand here and face him, but he was a man of his word, and that would earn her a spanking. She blinked, realizing that he'd been counting down.

"Five." He sat up straighter and pulled his shoulders back.

"Four."

He uncrossed his arms.

"Three."

Oh, God! It was now or never.

"Two."

He pushed himself to standing, making her heart thump wildly in her chest as she looked from side to side, desperate to get away, but hoping he wouldn't let her.

"One."

She ran to him.

Fuck it, she thought as his arms snaked her waist and he drew her to him just moments before he sat down on the couch, stood her in front of him, then bent her over his lap.

"Wait! Oh my God! Diego, what are you doing?" she asked, scissoring her legs in protest, her arms flailing. "You said you'd spank me if I didn't come to you! And I came! Jesus, I came!"

She felt him bunch the fabric of her skirt at the small of her back. She could only lay over his knee, unsure how to stop him and scared to push him away. "You'll listen to me, little girl," he clipped, now grasping the edge of her panties and pulling the silky fabric down over the rise of her ass and down her thighs, the smooth material caressing her as cool air graced her naked skin. "I told you I'd spank you if you didn't come to me, Nora. I never said I wouldn't if you did."

"That's—that's—so unfair! OW!" she screamed as his hand cracked down on her ass.

"You, young lady, have some explaining to do, and I think it's best done while over Daddy's knee."

She wriggled her backside, which only seemed to further encourage him, as he slapped her ass again. "If you think after the night we had I'm going to let you just take off out of here, you've got another think coming," he said, punctuating his words with a hard *crack* of his palm. "Now that I've got your undivided attention? Fucking *talk.*"

She lay over his knee, the handful of swats only making her hot and bothered all over again. "I-I started getting scared," she said.

"Scared of what?" he asked, hand poised. "Now we're getting somewhere. Maybe you ought to be scared of *me*, of Daddy spanking your ass."

He paused, his hand resting on her fiery bottom, and the touch of his palm made her insides turn to mush. Her pussy throbbed, and she squirmed in embarrassment.

"Ow!" she screamed out loud as his palm cracked against her ass again.

"I asked you a question," he said, his voice harsh, corrective. "And when I ask a question, I want an answer!" Another smack landed.

"Yes, Daddy!" Her response was instinctive. She groaned out loud.

"Answer, Nora," he ordered.

"Scared of… of where this is going," she said. "For most of the time I've known you, I've tried to convince myself you were a criminal."

He growled. "Some might say I am. Go on."

"I-I just don't know what to expect. I started thinking maybe we have potential, you and I, but there are too many things that scare me. I want to trust you." And to her surprise, tears filled her eyes and her throat felt tight. A sob escaped her.

"Baby," he said, lifting her in his arms and dragging her over his lap so that her sore ass scraped along the rough fabric of his jeans. "Come here." He pulled her to his chest and kissed the top of her head. "Of course you're scared," he said. "You *ought* to be scared. I've done wicked things, Nora, things the pope himself couldn't forgive. My mama is rolling over in her grave." He laughed then, a mirthless chuckle that made her shiver. "But I'm the one who saved you when you were kidnapped, and even though back then you thought I was the bad guy, I was the one who wanted you safe. I've watched you for years, Nora. You've never really been alone. And I would take a bullet before I let anyone, *including me*, hurt you."

She wanted to believe him, but how did she know he spoke the truth? "Really?" she asked, running her fingers along the scruff of his beard.

"Yes, Nora," he said. "And I get being scared." His voice hardened. "But damned if I'm gonna let you run away. You don't run from me without telling me what the fuck is going on. Yeah?"

It was a fair request. "Yeah," she said. "But you *did* spank me and that makes twice now."

He chuckled again, but this was different, amused this time. "And you're telling me you didn't deserve those spankings? And really, honey, a few smacks to the ass hardly count as a spanking."

Her eyes widened, jaw dropped open, and her panties dampened between her thighs. "You don't call that a spanking?" she whispered. Holy *shit*. What *was* Diego capable of?

"I guess it's a spanking, yeah," he said, his mouth coming to whisper in her ear. "But you haven't really pushed Daddy yet, baby." He paused, one of his hands releasing her waist and traveling between her legs. His low voice traipsed along her skin. "Have you, Nora?" His fingers dipped below the edge of her panties. "If I touch you, will I find you wet for me?" he asked. Her head dropped back as she clutched him, her hips rising of their own accord. "I'll take that as a yes," he said, one finger dipping lower and slid between her folds. "*Madre de Dios,*" he swore. "Wet as fucking hell for me."

He stood then, lifting her in his arms only to lower her on the couch so her body hit the back, kneeling in front of her. He made short work of removing her panties as he bent her knees and draped them over his shoulders, lowering his mouth so that his hot breath fluttered between her thighs. She forgot to breathe as her fingers anchored onto his hair and his tongue stroked at her folds.

"Oh, God," she said, writhing, but he held her fast, alternating lazy laps of his tongue with rapid sucks, then releasing her only long enough to nip at her inner thighs. She screamed, but then he was at it again, sucking her clit, teasing her with the tip of his tongue until she was soaring, gasping for air, drowning as her heart raced and she screamed his name out loud, and as she came down from her climax, he was at it again, still sucking her, a second climax building on the first.

He pumped his fingers into her, his eyes glittering as his gaze fixed on hers.

"Let yourself go, Nora," he coaxed. "Such a good girl coming for me." She clutched the cushions on the couch, her head falling from side to side as he pumped, the pad of his thumb circling her clit. "Come on Daddy's fingers, baby," he ordered, and she shattered a second time, writhing as spasms of pleasure consumed her, wracking her body until she fell back on the couch, panting.

He got to his feet as she lay limply, and he reached for her, drawing her into his arms. "Come here, Norita," he murmured, falling heavily against the arm of the couch and tucking her up against his chest, the second time he held her, and this time her full weight fell against him.

"Such a good girl, coming for Daddy," he said, moving her damp hair off her forehead and tucking it behind her ear.

She giggled at that, the afterglow fading now and she felt a bit embarrassed. "Yikes, that was hot," she said. "I never… I haven't ever…" she faltered.

"Shh, honey," he said.

She looked around the room in the stillness, then, enjoyed being held. Yes, there were scary things that really freaked her out about him and whoever he associated with, but didn't everyone have a dark side to them? Why was he so different? Aware that she was trying to justify her feelings for him, maybe not the wisest thing to do in the afterglow of sex, she shoved all thoughts of what was *right* and what was *good* away. He was holding her and it was all that mattered.

Her eyes drifted closed. She wanted to sleep as he held her in the silence. "Do you need a nap, honey?" he asked. "You seem tired."

"Mmm," she murmured. "Naps are good. But no, not now, because I'm starving and then I really need to get to work. I have a meeting with Diana this afternoon to go over the final plans for the fundraiser."

He chuckled and kissed the top of her forehead. "All right, then. This is what we do. You call and check in with everyone at work, we go get something to eat, we go to *Centered* for a bit, and then when we come back this afternoon, I'm putting you down for a nap." She squirmed, yet her heart fluttered.

"Putting me down for a nap? I'm not *that* tired," she protested, stifling a yawn that threatened to give her away. She'd been putting in extra hours at work, covering for a girl on vacation, and at home she'd been working hard at preparing for the big fundraising event. "And anyway, isn't that what you do for kids? I'm not a child." The protest was feeble, and she couldn't deny that she liked when he watched out for her, but she felt she owed it to womankind to defend herself.

"Naps aren't just for kids," he said, his voice deepening and taking on an authoritative edge. "And if your daddy thinks you need one, then you'll do what Daddy says." He reached for her ass that still stung and squeezed. "Won't you?" The implied threat made her squirm again. *Do what Daddy says or I'll spank you.* She bit her lip, and her eyes fluttered open, taking in the large expanse of his muscled chest, the strong arms that held her, his jawline with the scruffy beard.

"Yes, Daddy," she said, burying her head again lest he see her embarrassment. This was all so weird, yet so fucking hot and somehow, oddly, sweet.

He sat up straighter and swung her legs onto the floor. "Let's get something to eat," he said. Her stomach growled in response as she righted herself, smoothing her skirt and looking once more at the small picture on the mantle, more details apparent now that she stood a bit closer. The boy was grinning, his dark eyes so much like Diego's. He wore a dark green t-shirt and shorts, and sat on a swing, and it looked like he was mid-flight, with his older, taller siblings surrounding him. She reasoned he'd have been the youngest of his brothers and sisters. So tragic, to lose the life of such a little, innocent boy, she thought. No wonder Diego looked haunted at times, as if he couldn't rest until he'd seen to the final justice of those he pursued. She shook her head. It was time to go.

She freshened up and grabbed her bag he'd retrieved from her car, made a quick call to *Centered* to let them know she'd be in after lunch, then followed Diego as he led her out the door, giving her instructions. "Head down, Nora," he said, and for once, she wanted to obey him, and not because she feared he'd spank her ass.

He needed this, needed someone to protect and care for. "You don't look to the street or up, and you stay on the inside of the sidewalk, just like this. Don't hold my hand or get too close, just walk as if you've got nothing better to do, and get into the passenger side. Yeah?"

"Yeah," she whispered, doing exactly what he said. He opened the door for her, and as she slid into the car, he got into the driver's seat and hit a button on his phone.

"All clear," he said. "No one tailing us, far as I can tell, but I'll watch until we get on the highway. Send your man home." A pause. "Yeah, thanks, brother."

He clicked his phone off and tossed it in the console as he revved the engine, not offering her any further information. She could surmise, though, that he'd just given Slay's man permission to take off.

She shivered in her seat, attracted to the fact that other men obeyed him, did his bidding without question.

"You like pizza?" he asked. "Little Italian joint in the North End makes amazing pizza."

"Yeah, sure," she said. He drove along the street quietly, as her mind teemed with questions.

Who exactly did he work with? *How* would he bring this whole organization down? And what did that innocent girl back at *Centered* have to do with all of this?

"What's on your mind, Nora?" he asked, as he flicked on his directional and glanced at the rearview mirror. "No one following," he muttered.

"Lots of things," she said. "Too many to say out loud."

"Try me."

"If I push, I'm afraid you'll spank me," she said, surprising even herself when the words tumbled out of her mouth.

His lips quirked at the edges, and he reached across the seat for her hand, placing his larger, warm hand in hers on her knee as he spoke. "Oh, I fully intend on spanking you often," he said, in mock seriousness. "Don't tell me you don't like it." Her heartbeat spiked, and she drew her knees together. Hell yeah, she liked it. "But I'll only punish you if you disobey me. I won't spank you for asking questions, Nora."

She frowned, unsure how she felt about his punishing her. She couldn't even talk to her big sister about it, because Tessa was a submissive. She thrived on obedience and discipline, and though she'd been told Tessa and her husband Tony had a milder dynamic than the rest of them, she knew Tessa did have a few rules. The girls she knew firsthand from The Club were not weak but strong women, who willingly obeyed their dominants.

"Talk to me, Nora," Diego demanded, his voice lower now, stern, as he still held his hand over hers.

"I just don't get this whole thing is all," she said with a shrug. "I mean… I have a college education. I practically run a shelter for women, and I'm sitting here next to a guy telling me he'll punish me if I disobey him."

He shrugged. "Nothing wrong with that. You ought to know by now that guys like me like control. That's how some of us operate. The only question is, do you like giving up that control?"

Well, if that didn't sum it up right there. Huh.

"I don't know," she said, but she knew even now that if she did something stupid that put herself in danger, he would spank her whether she consented or not, and the knowledge made her pussy pulse.

God, she was so fucked up.

"Here we are," he said. "No one followed us, I know. Still, we'll go to the furthest corner inside. Sit where I tell you, because I need to be in a place where I can see the door."

"Are we on a date?" she asked as he held her hand and walked to a wrought iron table with two chairs in the corner of the square-shaped dining area.

"Call it whatever you want, honey," he said with a smirk. "I just know that soon I'm bringing you home to my bed. Do people usually date before that?" His grin deepened. "Okay then, this is a date."

She laughed out loud then. She wanted to go home with him, needed him to take her to bed. Her belly dipped in anticipation, her thighs clenched, and her mouth grew dry. God. Bed with Diego. He'd made her come repeatedly now, but still, she longed for the deeper connection with him.

He pulled a chair out and gestured for her to sit down, but his eyes weren't on her, they were on the doorway, then the windows, before they rested on a couple three tables away, who sat with a small child in a high chair. Nora sat down.

"Everything okay?" she asked, her brows furrowing as she placed her fabric napkin in her lap. He glanced again at the door, then the windows, then the couple.

"Yeah," he said. "For now." His eyes met hers again briefly, before he began scanning the room again and finally settled on his menu.

She leaned in closer to him. "Seriously, Diego. No one followed us. You don't always have to be on the lookout."

He placed the menu down, reached for her hand and squeezed. "But I do, Nora. I do."

Chapter 5

"Here's the deal," Diego told Nora, once they were back in the car. "I'm taking you to *Centered* because I know you have a job to do, and because I know Slay guards the place like Fort Knox. But you need to take extra precautions, because things have changed..."

She sighed. "You mean because of what we did last night?"

"Partly," he said, feeling his serious expression twist into a self-satisfied one, and not giving a damn. "But also because of what *you* did last night, just coming to see me."

She pursed her lips like she wanted to argue. "Diego, isn't it possible that you're overreacting just a little bit? I mean, *yes*, in retrospect it was a stupid thing for me to come looking for you last night. I don't really know what I thought I'd accomplish," she admitted. "Maybe it was just the shock of seeing Camila draw your face, of knowing you were involved with this girl somehow. And I wanted to make sure that you were okay."

He started the engine and backed out of the parking spot without glancing in her direction, though her words settled warmly in his stomach. How long had it been since someone wanted to make sure he was okay? Slay worried about him—he'd said as much the other day—but that was more about Diego's ability to do the job without losing his soul in the process. Diego couldn't remember someone worrying about whether he was upset or unhappy. And while he was perfectly capable of taking care of his own shit, it was still nice to think that someone—specifically *his Nora*—cared.

Still, it seemed that even after *two* spankings in less than twenty-four hours, his woman didn't understand the seriousness of the situation.

"Coming to find me *was* a stupid thing to do. But I'm not overreacting," he told her flatly, navigating his car through the narrow, crowded streets with practiced ease.

Out of the corner of his eye, he saw her eyes narrow at his quick agreement. She licked her lips like she was weighing her next words carefully. He nearly chuckled.

"I'm just saying, you have to admit that it's extremely unlikely that I've somehow gotten my picture on somebody's hit list just because I went to see you. People do walk in that neighborhood occasionally, and park there too. You got me out of there before any of your guys saw me. You took me back to your mom's house for the night, and you said you'd take care of moving my car. I think you're being just a little bit paranoid."

He darted a glance in her direction, one eyebrow raised, and she hastily tacked on a respectful, "*Daddy.*"

He blew out a breath. "Nora, baby, I find myself in a shitty position here. I can't tell you about the things that I'm involved in. Once again, not just *won't*, but *can't*, okay? You knowing that I'm undercover already means that my life is in your hands," he reminded her, and he heard her suck in a breath at his words. "Beyond that, investigations are ongoing, for one thing, and for another, the less you know, the less jeopardy you're in. But you're smart enough to realize, I think, that I am not the highest guy on the food chain, yeah? There are bigger predators in the waters than me?"

She nodded slowly.

"Okay. Then you need to understand that the person I work for—the organization I'm investigating—they have spies everywhere. Eyes watching *everywhere*. Ears fucking listening *everywhere*. I sweep this car twice a day for bugs and tracking devices. The house you were in earlier? My mother's house? I own it, but it's not in my own name and nobody knows it's mine. And still, Nora? Still, Slay or one of his guys sweeps the place every couple of days."

"But *why?*" she demanded, as they made their way out of the older, homier Italian neighborhood and through the bustling downtown, where late-lunching professionals thronged the sidewalks, enjoying the fall sunshine. "Daddy, you can't live in fear every day. I had to learn that myself, after what happened with Roger. I was jumpy for a *long* while, startling at every shadow or loud noise. I didn't want to leave the house, didn't want to see my friends. I did nothing but study. Tony loved it at first," she said, rolling her eyes as she thought of her loving but overprotective brother-in-law. "My grades were better than ever. But then he and Tess realized it wasn't healthy for me to be so worried. They took me to a therapist who helped me develop some coping strategies, and—"

"It's not the same thing, baby," Diego interrupted gently. "I'm glad you got the help you needed. I'm grateful that your sister and Tony got that for you, but this isn't the same thing. Back then, you were on high-alert and you didn't need to be. You needed to figure out how to convince your mind that it wasn't fight-or-flight time anymore."

"Right," she agreed.

"But for me? Nora, for me, it is *always* fight-or-flight time," he told her, and the words came out sadder than he'd imagined they would. "There are literally dozens of people in Boston who want me dead right now, or who *would* if they had any idea that I was undercover. So I have to be cautious *always*. And now that you're with me?" He reached over and grabbed her hand from where it rested against her thigh, pulling it atop the center console so she was anchored to him. "That means you're in danger, too. Just having you *physically* with me puts you in danger. But if they were ever to figure out what you mean to me? Even people I consider friendly wouldn't hesitate to use you to get to me."

Her fingers tightened on his momentarily.

"I might take chances with my own life, but I would never, ever risk yours."

"Diego… I—"

"Hush, baby," he told her firmly, brooking no resistance. "You had a question… a concern… and I've answered it. We aren't going to discuss it again. That's how this works, understand?"

She sucked in a breath, and he could almost hear the wheels in her head spinning as she thought of a suitable argument. But in the end, she surprised him by saying, "Yes, Daddy."

He brought their joined hands towards his mouth and kissed her knuckles. "Thank you, baby. I need to know that you'll do exactly what I tell you and take every precaution when I leave you at *Centered.*" The very thought of something happening to her was paralyzing.

He could sense her lingering hesitation and he smiled briefly. "I get that we are new at this. I get that this time yesterday, you wondered if I was a criminal… and maybe some part of you *still* has concerns," he added.

The blush on her cheeks confirmed his suspicion, and she darted a quick glance at him, as if to see if he was mad. But he wasn't, not at all. He believed that she trusted him to lead her, to never hurt her, and that was the most important thing. As for the rest? He'd rather have her cautious—and yes, fine, as suspicious of everyone as he was—than have her blindly following anyone.

"The fact that you are still going to do what I say, even if some part of you thinks I'm paranoid and crazy, that says a lot," he said quietly, and met her big, solemn brown eyes with his for a moment.

"I trust you," she told him. And even though she was only confirming his thoughts, he felt a knot loosen in his chest. He thought, once again, of how lost he'd felt yesterday. Now, holding her trust and being worthy of it was his anchor.

"Okay, so here's what's going to happen. I know you're gonna talk to your sister and your friends, but play it cool. There's no reason for you to mention me at all just yet. And definitely don't mention where you're going to be sleeping." She nodded, and he continued. "Slay and his team are going to be doing security at *Centered*, as usual. But today, they're also going to monitor inside the facility."

"*Inside?*" Nora repeated. "Diego, so many of our clients are domestic violence victims, and having a bunch of big, beefy guys…"

"Slay's doing it himself," Diego interrupted. "He's a known presence there, thanks to Allie, so the women are familiar with him. And the kids absolutely love him. Plus, Slay's got two women on his team who both volunteered."

"Women? Slay has *women* on his team?" Nora sounded skeptical, and Diego had no hesitation in setting her straight.

"Hell yes. Why wouldn't he? Slay only cares they're good at their jobs, and Nakima and Faith are both Krav Maga-trained badasses with law enforcement backgrounds. Besides, sometimes having someone who doesn't *look* like a scary badass gives us a competitive advantage. Nobody suspects just how scary they can be."

"I just thought…. He's always so protective of… I mean, because of Allie…" she stammered.

"Yeah, I know exactly what you thought," Diego teased. "That because Alice is submissive to him, clearly he must be a chest-beating caveman who wouldn't value women on his team? Slay has a protective streak a mile wide. So do I. But that doesn't mean I believe that *every* woman needs protecting in *every* situation."

She shook her head. "I know better. I mean, he's hyper-protective of me and the rest of the family, but I know Slay's not a caveman." She looked at Diego thoughtfully, and once again he could practically *hear* her thinking. He bit his cheek to keep from smiling. Even if he'd ever allowed himself to fantasize about a future where they were together, he would never have imagined something this *fun*.

"Spit it out," he told her, as he turned down the street that led to *Centered*.

She seemed startled that he'd read her thoughts. "Well, I was just thinking I've always wanted to learn Krav Maga. And if I put in some effort and became proficient, then you wouldn't have to be as protective of me."

He snorted, then laughed out loud. "Yeah, no."

"No? But you just said not every woman needs protecting! And if I know self-defense—"

"I don't care if you become the world's greatest Krav Maga master, *and* wear body armor from head to toe while locked in a hermetically sealed bubble on a tiny, uncharted island in the middle of the ocean. I'm *still* going to worry about you. I'm still going to need to protect you. And it's not because you're weak, Nora. I *know* you're not. Fuck, in some ways you're one of the strongest women I've ever met. It's for my own sanity." He reached over and grabbed her hand. Emotion was making his throat tight and he wondered for a second if he was saying too much, but she needed to hear it. She needed to understand. "You are infinitely precious to me. You always have been. I gave up a lot of things to do this job, and I always figured that having you in my life was one of them. Now that you're with me, I can't *not* protect you."

He deftly maneuvered the car into an empty spot just down the street from the bench where he'd watched her last night—*shit*, how was it only last night?—then killed the engine and shifted in his seat to face her. "It's my job now, baby. And it's also my joy. Taking care of you, knowing that *I* am the guy who gets to make sure you have every single thing you *need* and most of the things you *want*, that's about the best thing that's ever happened to me. Letting me do that, *helping* me do that, even when you think I'm being overly cautious, is the greatest gift that you can give me."

Her eyes were soft and warm as they locked on his. "Okay, baby?" he asked softly.

She bit her lip, but couldn't keep the smile from lighting up her face and stealing his breath.

"Okay, Daddy."

"FUCK. THIS IS BAD, PADRE," Juan whispered, his wide brown eyes shifting quickly from Diego to Tomás and back again. "El Jefe knows the girl left, and that means he's gonna come for us if we don't get her back?"

Diego leaned back in his chair and stared at the dozen faces gathered around the flimsy table his men had set up in the center of the warehouse. Most of the faces were held carefully blank, revealing nothing. Others, like Tomás, glared at him angrily. And a couple, like Ricky and Juan, looked like they were ready to piss themselves in fear.

He'd been reluctant to call the meeting for this very reason, wanting to take care of the situation without riling half his crew. But this morning, when he'd left Nora at his house and come to the warehouse to check on Ricky, he'd found Tomás waiting for him, demanding answers. It had become clear that if *Diego* didn't call the meeting, Tomás would do so himself, which showed exactly how strained Tomás's loyalty to him had become.

Diego squelched a pang of regret. There had been times when Tomás had felt like a brother to him over the years, and

Diego still felt an almost fraternal pull to protect and guide the younger man. But he now recognized just how fucked up his loyalties had become, and knew he should be grateful for Tomás's animosity. It would only make it easier for Diego to make a clean break, easier to bring down the whole fucking organization.

He sighed. "It's not gonna blow back on you, Juancho," he promised, holding the other man's gaze.

"Yeah?" Juan said nervously. His eyes darted around again like a scared rabbit, and Diego briefly wondered what the fuck the man was high on and how much of it he'd taken. "How can you be sure?"

Diego opened his mouth to reply, but Tomás responded before he could.

"He *can't*," Tomás challenged bitterly. "Padre doesn't *know* what El Jefe will do, and there ain't nothin' we can do to stop him, except get the girl back."

The grinding of Diego's molars was nearly audible in the silence that descended after that, as all eyes turned to him to gauge his response to the blatant challenge. A week ago... fuck, even a *day* ago, the need to maintain his position and his cover would have required Diego to make a demonstration, to make Tomás cower in fear and remind him that Diego was absolutely the strongest motherfucker in the room. But the ticking clock in the back of his head—*one week, no longer*—made that unnecessary. His only goal now was to bring down this group with as little bloodshed as possible. It was a liberating feeling.

He found himself genuinely smiling as he replied, "I'm gonna take care of this. El Jefe gave me a lead on where to find her. Consider it done." He looked at the men around the table again, and found that most of them had relaxed as they noticed his calm demeanor, a couple even leaning back in their chairs.

But Tomás was unconvinced. "Yeah? You gonna share your

brilliant plan with the class?" He crossed his arms over his chest and stared Diego down.

"Fuck no," Diego told him mildly, refusing to be goaded into an angry response despite his overwhelming desire to run Tomás's smug face through the table and remind him to show respect. "The fewer people who know what's going on here, the fewer people can mess this shit up with their impulsive behavior." He looked pointedly at Ricky, who blinked his one good eye and flushed guiltily. "I'll get her."

"You don't need to *get* her, you need to *kill* her." Tomás challenged, and Diego's eyes flashed to his as the men around the table nodded in agreement.

You need to kill her. As simple as that? Since when had Tomás been able to discuss the cold-blooded killing of an innocent girl in such bold and unrepentant terms? Since when did the rest of the men agree so easily?

Suddenly, Diego didn't feel like he knew Tomás or the crew at all anymore. And that made it easier for him to lie through his teeth.

"I have a plan, but it's gonna require some preparation. If we don't want blowback, we don't go stalking up to her in broad daylight with guns blazing." He looked around at the men. "*Jesus.* Forget El Jefe's shitlist, we'd all be arrested for fucking murder. *Verdad*, Tomás?" The other man scowled and looked daggers at Diego, but nodded once. "Banyon, the police still haven't had any reports, right?"

"*Sí*, Padre. My contact in the PD says it's all good. Wherever the girl ended up, she was smart enough not to go reporting us to anyone. If there *is* a report, my contact will tip us off in plenty of time to take action."

Diego nodded. The girl—*Camila*, he reminded himself. She had a name, and he would use it, at least in his own mind—*wouldn't* report it. Not for a little while, at least. Diego, via Slay, had made sure of that. Slay had arranged a temporary home for her with his guy Donnie and Donnie's wife, Grace, who worked at *Centered*, because they needed to ensure that Camila was placed with someone who was able to adequately protect her from El Jefe. Diego had also tipped Slay off that, although Camila still needed to receive the services and counseling she could get through *Centered*, she needed to be there as infrequently as possible and to vary her arrival and departure times, so she was a difficult target.

"That's good. That gives us time. No *shipments* until next weekend," he told the men, their nods confirming they understood that meant no new girls should be arriving. "So in the meantime, we keep our heads down and conduct business as usual. Banyon, you and your crew keep unloading the legit merch at the warehouse, and take care of delivering it to our buyers." The souvenirs and novelty items they imported as a front for the darker side of their business still needed to be taken care of, after all.

Banyon and several others nodded.

"Ricky, you and the boys keep to your usual haunts—the pool hall and bars in and around here. Gather some intel, see what the other guys have to say. Last fucking thing we need is another crew looking into our shit while we're trying to deal with things internally, you feel me?"

"You got it, Padre," Ricky said, his voice subdued and respectful.

Diego smirked. "Meanwhile, I'm gonna handle this other project," he told them. "And, as I said, I'll do it alone."

Tomás sat forward, forearms on the table, and shifted his jaw to the side as he looked at Diego. "No, I still don't like it. You don't wanna tell *everyone*, fine. But you need to tell *some* of us what your plan is."

"Do I?" Diego's reply was soft and flat—his most dangerous tone, whether Tomás recognized it or not.

"You do," Tomás confirmed with a nod. "I mean, what if

something should happen to *you* while you're taking care of things? This is a dangerous business, Padre. You need backup."

Diego's gut clenched as he stared at Tomás, processing the thinly-veiled threat in the man's words. So Tomás planned to make a play for the throne, huh? He wanted Diego out? Well, Tomás didn't know it, but Diego would be out soon enough. But in the meantime, an idea took shape in Diego's mind… a way to set a trap for the man he'd once considered a friend that would protect him from El Jefe and bring him to justice, all at once.

"Have it your way," Diego agreed. "I'm happy to share information with you. I'll text you all the details and anything new I learn." He saw suspicion flare in Tomás's eyes at this easy capitulation and almost chuckled. He'd taught Tomás well in *some* ways, at least. "But hear me, man: You follow *my* lead. You do nothing without my authorization."

"Of course." Tomás smiled, but it wasn't friendly. "Padre."

Diego nodded, glancing around the table once more. Was this the last time he'd sit at this table with these men? It had been a long while since he'd let himself consider what the end of his assignment might look like. Years had passed and blood had been shed since then, but even back in the day, he'd expected the end might be bittersweet. A couple of days ago, it had felt downright impossible. But then Nora had come back into his life, widening his perspective and destroying the thick wall he'd erected around his heart. Now, he was so eager to get back to his woman and make sure she was okay, he could barely keep his feet from tapping impatiently. Only force of habit held him in his seat.

He rose abruptly. "*Hasta luego,*" he said. And then he looked each man, even Tomás, in the eyes. It hit him suddenly that if he ever saw them again, it would likely be from the opposite side of a courtroom, if anyone ever got enough evidence to really bring El Jefe down. These men would no longer look upon him as their brother, their leader, a man they'd take a bullet for, and who would take a bullet for them. Instead, they'd know him for the traitor he was.

He sucked in a sharp breath as his own words from yesterday came back to him. *Feel every second of that pain. This is the price of betrayal.*

"*Vaya con Dios,*" he told them softly, then he turned around and walked away.

"MY ETA IS FIVE MINUTES," Diego told Slay, holding the phone at his ear as he maneuvered his car through the busy streets of downtown Boston, keeping an eye on his rearview mirror to make sure he wasn't being tailed. "Traffic near the museum was crazy. And I took an extra minute to pull over and check the car for devices, too." He could imagine what Nora would call that level of extreme caution: *paranoia.* But whatever. He'd be cautious enough for both of them. "Anything happening over there?"

Slay understood that Diego didn't want the play-by-play, and he cut to the heart of Diego's question. "Nora's fine."

Diego's shoulders relaxed, though he hadn't been aware of how tense he was. "Good. Business as usual?"

"Yeah," Slay confirmed. "They're going crazy getting this fundraiser shit sorted, plus Elena had a meeting with a city counselor this afternoon. Alice and Nora have been busy smiling and showing some bigwig donors around." Disapproval and worry rang in his voice. "Despite the fact that my wife is carrying another ten-pound Slater male."

"Another boy?" Diego asked. "Congrats, man. I thought you guys weren't finding out until the big day."

"We're not *officially,*" Slay confirmed. "But this isn't my first rodeo. Between Allie, Elena, and the other women, I think I'm qualified to write a book on this shit. This kid is kicking twice as much as the twins did together, keeping Allie up all night. It's definitely another son, and he's gonna keep his big brothers on their toes!"

Diego shook his head. Slay might be psychic about a lot of things, but Diego wasn't so sure he'd put money on this particular prediction.

Slay continued, "Anyway, it's not good for Alice to be on her feet so much at this stage of the game. I want her to cut back her hours once this fundraiser is done, and maybe the two of us will duck out entirely for a little vacation before the baby comes. I kinda guessed from your call this morning that I wouldn't have a problem finding a man to take security shifts here, now that you have a *vested interest* in keeping this place as safe as possible. So can I write your name in the schedule?" he teased.

Damn it. Diego had specifically avoided giving Slay any information beyond the basics during their briefing call that morning. *Nora may have gotten herself on El Jefe's radar last night, and he was putting her in a safe house. Could Slay arrange for someone to collect some clothes from her place? Oh, and Nora's car was parked off Border Street. Could Slay send someone to get it?* Figured the nosy fucker had already worked out there was only once place Diego would consider Nora truly safe, and that was with Diego himself. But how had Slay realized that this was going to be permanent, that things between him and Nora had changed?

"Your woman's been smiling like a loon all afternoon," Slay said quietly, before Diego could even formulate the question. "Pretty much happier than I've ever seen her. Doesn't take an investigator to piece the facts together, brother."

Diego cleared his throat but otherwise said nothing, and Slay laughed harder. "Yup. Definitely putting your name down for *Centered* detail. Otherwise you'll be harassing whichever guy I assign, and I'll have people quitting left and right."

Diego rolled his eyes. He would not *harass* his coworkers.

Much.

Whatever.

"Already have an assignment," Diego told Slay. "Or did you forget?"

"Hard to forget," Slay muttered. "Considering I attempted a conversation with Camila myself this morning and saw exactly what life in El Jefe's realm has done to her. But after what the bastard told you on the phone today, that's a moot point. I'm not risking you any further, Diego." Slay took a deep breath and said, "It's time to tie your shit up and get out."

Diego pulled his car into the tiny private lot behind *Centered*. He killed the engine, and sat staring at the brick wall that ringed the enclosure. It *was* time to get out. His hand had been forced by the situation with Camila and El Jefe's ultimatum. His failure to bring the organization down despite all the shit he'd had to do and the sacrifices he'd made over the years left a bitter taste in his mouth, but his future with Nora was more important

"I have a couple of loose ends to tie up, a couple things to talk to you about. But I've said my goodbyes."

Slay grunted. "Glad to hear it."

"You gonna let me in the building or what?" Diego demanded, pulling himself out of the car and locking it before making his way to the rear entrance of the building.

"On my way down now," Slay said. A moment later the door opened and Slay stood in the doorway, sliding his phone in his pocket.

Diego put his own phone away and held up his hand for Slay to take. "S'up?"

"Listen, the fancy suits are still here," Slay said, rolling his eyes. "It's some walkthrough thing so they can get their donation fingers prepped to write lots of zeroes at the end of their checks on Saturday." He led Diego down the basement hallway, past a few storage rooms and mechanical closets, to a narrow set of stairs.

"These stairs lead to the hallway in front of Nora's office," Slay continued. "Two floors up. When you open the stairway door, her office is the first one on the left. You'll see her name on it. Probably for the best if we don't have you skulking through the halls, at least not while we know El Jefe has eyes on this place. Once we make sure 'Diego Santiago' has disappeared for good, and El Jefe has stopped looking for you, it'll be a different story." He turned to look at Diego. "Thought about a new name?"

Diego shook his head. "Haven't gone down that road yet," he told Slay. "New name, new identity, all to hide from that fucking psychopath El Jefe because I couldn't get the job done? It burns just a little." He thought of the people who had shared his name —his mother, his brother. Yeah, it burned a fuck of a lot.

Slay nodded somberly and clapped him on the shoulder. "I'm not gonna get all touchy feely or whatever, but there's a lot you'll never be able to tell people about this assignment. I'm one of the few who'll ever know the details. So, just to say, I appreciate what you've sacrificed for this."

Diego felt his cheeks heat. "It's my job."

"Yeah," Slay agreed, his light brown eyes on Diego's. "It is. And it's also *not*. So just fucking accept my gratitude. You've made us all safer by doing what you've done."

Jaw tight, throat working, he remembered his first meeting with Slay all those years ago. It felt like a different time. Like he'd been a different person. Diego nodded and accepted Slay's words.

Slay clapped him on the shoulder again. "I'll ask one of the volunteers to find Nora and let her know her office is occupied," he said, moving off towards another set of stairs further down the hall.

Diego opened the stairwell door and climbed the dimly-lit stairs to the second-floor landing, but before he could pull open the door and find Nora's office, he heard voices coming down the hallway. Heeding Slay's warning, he ducked into the shadowy corner of the stairwell, where he wouldn't be seen from the window in the door. He rolled his eyes at himself. How many years had he spent undercover? And yet the first time he'd been forced to literally duck into a dark corner was the day he'd decided to step out into the light.

The voices paused just on the other side of the door, outside what must have been Nora's office.

"I must say, I'm impressed, Nora." The speaker was clearly a woman, her voice husky and cultured, with a hint of a Spanish accent. "You've done excellent work here. And your plans for the fundraiser are spectacular. Your talent and passion for helping these women are extraordinary."

"Oh. Wow. Thank you so much, Diana," Nora replied, and he could hear the self-conscious smile in her voice. Diana was the woman she'd mentioned before, the one who was her mentor and champion. Curiosity about the woman had his ears perking up. "I-I *think* we have everything well in hand. Flyers are printed, volunteers are in place, catering is locked down…"

"I knew you were more than capable of handling this," Diana said. "Or I wouldn't have asked you to take on something of this scope. Just think of how many lives you'll change for the better on Saturday." There was warm pride in her voice, like Nora was her own daughter, and Diego smiled.

"That's what I'm most excited about, helping the women who…" Nora began. "Oh! Speaking of the women, I almost forgot! You remember the reporter who's going to do a profile on the fundraiser, Gretchen Liu? She asked me to verify contact information with you for Paolina and Ruth Castronieves, as well as Petra Alexandrovich. None of them have answered her calls or emails."

Diana hesitated. "I'm sorry. Who?"

"Paolina, Ruth, and Petra?" Nora paused expectantly, then explained further. "The women you got jobs for? Down in Miami?"

"Oh! Yes, yes, yes. Of course!! I'm getting old, *mija*," Diana complained, and Nora giggled. "Names, dates, it's all a jumble. *I* contact *people* for information, not the other way around."

Diego blinked as a feeling of déjà vu washed over him. Where had he heard that before? Slay, maybe? Or…

"Okay, first, you're not *old*," Nora argued. "You're gorgeous and brilliant."

Diana laughed, low and rich. "Gorgeous *and* brilliant? Oh, *mija*, you're good for my ego!"

"I'm serious! And the way you mentor other women—like Paolina and Ruth and Petra and *me*—is pretty darn inspirational," Nora said staunchly. "It's rare enough that a woman runs a business that has a presence in almost every major city on the east coast—Boston, New York, Philly, D.C., Atlanta, Miami. But you didn't just amass a big pile of money, no! You turned around and figured out ways you could give back! You got involved *personally*. You looked at women who were vulnerable, who'd run out of options, and you relocated them and got them jobs."

Nora's voice was practically vibrating with emotion, but Diego's blood had gone cold. He and Slay's team had investigated practically every major businessman in the city of Boston who had the means to run the kind of operation that El Jefe ran —those who had ties in multiple major cities, including an active presence in Boston and Miami, and had a multifaceted operation where regular shipments wouldn't raise red flags on government shipping manifests.

But had they investigated business*women*?

He shook his head. There was a reason why they'd all unconsciously ignored any women-run businesses. How likely was it that the mastermind of a fucking sex trafficking ring, a ring of criminals who preyed almost exclusively on *women*, was a woman herself?

Pretty freakin' unlikely.

Was this the kind of over-cautiousness Nora had been talking about this morning? Another example of his suspicious nature, a paranoia he'd gained from years of living undercover? The woman, Diana, had been nothing but helpful to Nora and, for all he knew, to many, many underprivileged women over the years. He had to be barking at shadows. *Didn't he?*

Diana's cell phone rang, cutting off whatever her reply might have been, and Nora whispered, just loud enough for Diego to hear, "I'll just step into my office while you take that."

A second later, Diana was speaking into her phone in rapid Spanish. "I told you not to call except in an emergency… Contact? From who? Ahhh. Well, that *is* surprising. So he thinks he can double cross me?"

Diego smiled grimly. Seemed Diana wasn't just a philanthropist; she could be ruthless too, when necessary. He pressed his back to the cool cement wall and listened closely.

"He's *out*. You understand what I'm saying? Out. Permanently. Make it fucking happen, Miguel."

Miguel. A common enough name. But Diego's pounding heart remembered all too well where he'd last heard that name spoken. *From El Jefe's phone*, and in nearly the same tone. *Shit.* If it was true… Who would ever imagine?

But hadn't he just talked with Nora about this today? About Slay employing women who were competent for the job precisely because they *deflected suspicion?* How had none of them considered this possibility before?

He heard Diana knock gently on Nora's office door before she stepped inside with a soft laugh. Part of him wanted to run in there right now, gun drawn, and remove his woman from the room, but he had no concrete evidence, only coincidences. A fuck-ton of coincidences, to be sure, but not nearly enough to prove to Nora that the woman she viewed as a mentor could be a criminal. He would need more proof before he could convince her—or, hell, *anyone*, that Diana could somehow be… El Jefe.

He gave one last hard glance at the door to the hallway, then forced himself to take the stairs back down a level before sliding his phone out of his pocket and redialing his last call.

"Slay?" he said, before the other man could greet him. "I lied. I'm not ready to pull out quite yet. One last avenue to explore, and it's fucking crazy, man, but just go with me here. Listen…"

Then he proceeded to share his suspicions with Slay, growing colder and more convinced with the retelling.

Chapter 6

Nora shut and locked the door at *Centered*, smiling to herself when she saw Diego come up behind her peripherally. "Lurking in the shadows, huh?" she teased. He hadn't really been lurking in the shadows but he had been there all day, and the day before that, and the day before that. Though she knew he'd come and gone at various times based on her shift, and he never actually interacted with anyone at *Centered*, he was keeping a close eye on her and everyone else who worked there, as was Slay.

"Skulking around like a kid who shoplifted a candy bar," he said, removing his hands from his pockets as he drew closer to her. His hands spanned her waist, the warmth of his mouth at her ear, his whole body behind her warming her. She shivered. Tonight, they had plans to go back to his place. Between his schedule and hers, they hadn't been alone together in a few days, and she was eager for the privacy.

"Naughty, naughty," she said, pocketing the key and turning toward him. He leaned down and kissed her briefly before taking her hand. His car was only a few paces away.

He clicked his key fob, opened the door, and waited until she was in safely before shutting the door behind her. When her door was shut, he glanced over his shoulder, tensed for a moment as if convincing himself danger didn't lurk in the shadows, then went to the driver's side and slid in.

"Hungry, baby?" he asked pulling onto the main road.

"Starving," she said. "The girls at *Centered* were ordering food for lunch but I had a meeting with Diana, and didn't want to be interrupted."

From the corner of her eye, she watched as his jaw clenched. Was he angry with her that she hadn't eaten dinner? An uber protective guy like him wanted to be sure his girl was taken care of, just like the other guys in her circle of friends often did. Her heart tripped in her chest as she adjusted her bag in her lap.

"Another meeting with Diana? Tell me about this woman," Diego said, his voice shifting from daddy to commander.

Nora smiled. Diana had taken her under her wing, and she loved her. "I only met her face to face a few months ago—it was the first time *any* of us had met her. Before then, we'd only talked to her on the phone or emailed. She's an advocate for women's rights, and has championed for abused women for decades now. She's a successful businesswoman, and invests a great deal of time and money in *Centered*." Nora paused, aware that she was gushing now and that Diego had straightened beside her.

"Why would a smart, successful businesswoman like her invest time and money in a place like *Centered*?" he asked, frowning, as he took a turn.

Nora frowned, and her joy at recounting her experience with Diana evaporated. Everywhere Diego went, he saw ghosts, and now he was asking probing questions about Diana? Her mentor? The only mother-figure she'd ever had?

Nora's defenses went up as she stared at him. "Because she's a good person!" she replied, noting that her voice sounded a bit defensive. "You think it's a waste of time for someone to invest in the future of abused women?"

He raised an eyebrow in her direction. "I'm just asking, *mija*. I don't question that *Centered* is worth the time and effort. If I did, would I encourage the work you do?"

She frowned. Well, no. He continued. "Just not sure what's in it for her."

Nora inhaled with practiced patience. "Diana's *lovely*, Diego. So sweet. Tessa loves her."

He merely frowned. "Listen, honey. I admire the work you do. Honestly. And I know you girls have worked hard to make it a safe place. I just have some concerns about Diana. No one really knows who she is, and I wonder if she's trustworthy." He reached a hand out and placed it gently on her bare knee. "You put a lot of trust in her, and I need to know that trust is well-placed. I just want what's best for you, Norita," he said, and with that, her heart softened a bit.

"I know you do," she replied, placing her hand atop his. "Thank you, Daddy."

She looked out the window, still self-conscious of calling him daddy. She'd worked so hard to be a respected professional, and she wondered how her clients and co-workers would react if they knew she was attracted to a man who called himself daddy. But as she thought about it, she realized she didn't much care. It felt nice to have someone care about her, to have someone she could trust. Someone who would watch over her. Besides, it gave her a little zing of excitement every time.

As he threaded his way through the lines of traffic, she remembered the one time Tessa had ever taken her to the Boston Theater District. They'd seen a play, something about bootleggers and Prohibition, but the actual play had faded from her memory. What she remembered was the song the lead actress sang, longing and need in her voice as it echoed in the small theater. Gershwin's lyrics had burned into Nora's heart and memory.

. . .

SOMEONE TO WATCH OVER ME...

SHE PLAYED the words over in her head, as she thought about Diego. What would Tessa say? Was a part of her attracted to him because he was dangerous, ruthless even? Or was it something more? She had hinted to Tessa in recent texts that she'd been seeing Diego, but they hadn't talked about it at length yet. Diego had allowed for her telling Tessa, but she hadn't quite been up for the conversation yet.

"Let's get some food, baby," Diego said, coming to a stop at a small market. "Then after we eat?" He paused, his eyes smoldering as he looked to her and squeezed her hand. "I'm taking you home."

Her palms grew sweaty and her belly clenched, a low pulse in her belly responding to his voice. She watched him as he walked to help her out of the car. God, she was so hopelessly attracted to him and at that moment, she didn't care why.

"Come on." He ducked in the doorway to the little store, and pulled her through behind him, grabbing a basket. He selected a few ready-made sandwiches, some sparkling water, and a bag of chips, then tossed in a small plastic bowl of ripe strawberries.

"We'll have a picnic," he said.

"On your couch?" she responded with a laugh.

He grinned wickedly. "No, baby. On my bed."

Nora gasped. "Someone could've heard you!" she hissed. He merely shrugged and winked.

"Can I just wait in the car?" she asked, wanting to run and hide so no one could see her flushed cheeks. "Seriously, if you know what you want, I can just—"

His eyes sobered and his brow furrowed. "No."

Suddenly, she wanted to defy him, to tell him he couldn't tell her what to do, but his eyes narrowed on her. "Going to push me, Nora?" he asked, shaking his head. "Pretty sure you know how

I'd handle that, honey." He raised a brow, and at the same time, shoved a freezing cold can of whipped cream in her hand. "You take that. I'm gonna need it later. Take this to the checkout." He chuckled as her mouth dropped open, shifted the food basket to his left hand and before she knew what was happening, he gave her a teasing swat with the right.

Her pulse spiked, and her lips thinned as she fought to get her shit together.

"What was that?" she hissed at him, shocked he'd spanked her ass in public, and reluctantly impressed that he had.

He leaned in and whispered in her ear. "That, honey, was me reminding you to behave yourself." Her heart skipped a beat, and she swallowed hard. Part of her wanted to fight him, to tell him he had no business manhandling her where others could see, but she knew that if she did fight him, it would draw even more attention to them. And she also knew she didn't really want him to stop. She flushed as he paid for the groceries, then followed him as he led her to the car, opening her door for her.

"Okay, Nora," he said, getting in the driver's seat and heading toward the intersection. "Let's have a little talk."

As she looked over at him, curious what he wanted to talk about, she traced the leather edge of his seat with her fingernail. "What is it?" she asked, her stomach knotted in anticipation. Having grown up with an alcoholic mother, she often felt guilty anticipation when someone questioned her. And this was a guy who was over-the-top dominant, sexy as sin, and made her call him daddy.

"I'm planning on taking you to bed tonight," Diego said, his eyes still focused on the road but his spine going ramrod straight, his lips tight as he drove.

Her heart fluttered in anticipation, as her mind raced. "Oh?" she asked. "Is that right?"

He raised a brow in her direction before looking back at the main road, and she closed her eyes briefly before responding.

"Yes, Daddy," she said, enjoying how it felt, the sweet mingling of comfort and arousal, suddenly overwhelmed by the need to be held by him.

In bed with Diego Santiago. She couldn't believe her wildest teenage fantasies were coming true.

He cleared his throat and flicked his directional as she gazed at him from the side. His lean, muscled chest stretched the t-shirt he wore, bulging at his biceps, tapering down to a trim waist and jeans that hugged his hips. His dark, longish hair hung about his face, and his jaw sported several days' growth.

Her pussy clenched and she splayed a hand across her chest, but when she realized what she was doing, she pretended to scratch an itch on her neck. His large, powerful hands gripped the steering wheel, one finger tapping a rhythm. "Nora, are you on birth control?" he asked.

She nodded her head. Though it was the last thing she expected him to talk about, it was something that needed to be discussed. "Yes," she said, and when he raised a stern brown, she amended, "Daddy."

Her pulse quickened as she smoothed her hands along her thighs. She hadn't considered that Diego wouldn't want to use condoms, but the thought of him bare inside her thrilled her. The bigger question was, how would she handle sex with Diego? Would he be as sweet as he was now, or did he switch on the dom when he had her behind closed doors? Would he be a gentle lover, or would he simply take her? She replayed the past few times things had gotten hot and heavy and decided... not a gentle lover. Though, perhaps he could be if he wanted to. The three carefully-chosen men she'd slept with in the past had all been gentle, almost timid, and had been perfectly fine letting her remain in control. She knew Diego would be different. Her pulse kicked up at the mere thought.

When he didn't respond at first, she began to grow nervous. "Um... Diego? That isn't the answer you were looking for?" she asked. "I don't understand. We have to use birth control." Why was he probing? Her defenses rose.

"Were you wondering if I was a virgin?" she asked. "Is that what this was about?" When he didn't answer at first, her mind began to go haywire and she found herself snapping. "You're worried that because I'm on birth control I've been sleeping around?"

He shook his head. "Relax, baby."

She took a calming breath. She knew she was being unreasonable. Her mother had always screamed at Tessa for having boyfriends, and Nora remembered the horrid way her mother hurled insults at her, calling her a slut and a whore, and when Nora started dating, she'd gotten the same treatment.

"Sorry," she said. "My mom was always on my case about who I dated, and the second we were with a guy who she thought was above us or whatever, she started calling us whores and telling us we just wanted their money."

He didn't say anything at first, and when he finally spoke, his voice was controlled. "I remember your mother," he said. Diego had been to the shitty little apartment where she'd grown up. He'd seen the coffee table where her mother and her loser friends snorted lines. He'd seen her mother's boyfriends passed out on the recliner.

He knew where she'd come from. But how much did he know? Did he know that when she was a kid, her cupboards were bare and Tessa had worked behind the scenes with the counselor at her elementary school to get Nora free breakfast and lunch? Did he know that Tessa worked little jobs whenever she could as a teen, getting cash from the landlord for weeding his garden because their mother drank every penny of her income?

She didn't realize her hands were shaking until one of his came to rest on hers. "Hush, honey," he said. "I didn't mean to upset you. I just needed to know if I needed to buy protection is all. That's why I asked. I'm not judging anything."

"Yeah," she said softly, her heartbeat slowing as his thumb gently circled her hand. "Just when I think I've dealt with that shit, it just comes right back to bite me in the ass," she mumbled.

He squeezed her hand, turning onto the street that led to his house. "Shit like that you don't just deal with, honey. Sometimes, it haunts you." He grew quiet, and didn't offer any more as he pulled in front of the house.

What were *his* ghosts? What were the things that came back to haunt him?

"Did you grow up poor, like me?" she asked. "What were your parents like?"

He didn't answer at first as he cut the engine. "We weren't rich," he said. "But we did okay. My mom worked two jobs and so did my dad. There were a bunch of us, and I took on a lot of responsibility early. My dad died when I was twelve. When I was eighteen, my younger brother Armando got recruited to Salazar's organization, and I decided to join too, to keep him safe. I was always watching out for my siblings-like a parent. Not that it mattered. He died, and it was too much for my mom to handle. She died a year later. Heart failure. The rest of my siblings moved as far away from this town as they could, but I kept the house so that they'd always know they could come home." He shrugged a shoulder, his eyes teasing her. "I think I learned how to boss people around real young."

She snorted. "Shocker."

He playfully slapped her thigh, then opened his door. "Let's go inside and eat, honey. I'm starving. But listen, Nora. You don't worry about that shit that haunts you. You face it. And when you do, you realize that it doesn't define you. Got it?"

Her throat tightened and she could only nod. She wondered if Diego understood that about himself.

Dusk had fallen, and the chill fall air made her shiver. As he glanced over his shoulder, first to the left, then to the right, she felt better knowing she was beside a guy who would take care of her. Even if there was danger lurking in the shadows, she could trust him to protect her. He stood on the edge of the sidewalk nearest the street, holding her hand and pulling her close to him, as they both put their heads down against the biting wind. It wouldn't be long now before they'd have their first frost, and shortly after that, snow would begin to fly. She thought of all the women in Boston who they wanted to help, woman after woman coming into *Centered* for whatever they needed. She thought of what they'd do over the cold winter months, and how she'd have to work overtime when they saw an influx of people who didn't have shelter.

She shivered at a particularly cold gust of wind, and Diego drew her closer to him. He was warm, protective, and strong, almost making her forget the conversation she'd had in the car with him. She hated remembering her childhood and her mother. She wished she could erase it all from her memory and fill her head with peaceful thoughts instead.

What lurked in his mind? What kept him up at night? She shivered again. What did years of rubbing shoulders with evil do to a man?

He opened the front door for her, and she stepped inside. He scanned to the left and right and then back again, giving an almost imperceptible nod as if this somehow alleviated his concerns.

Would he always be troubled by shadows?

He shut and locked the door, then took the bags of groceries from her and tossed them down on the kitchen counter. Turning around, he leaned against the counter, spreading his legs wide and opening his arms. She met his eyes, warming as he looked her way. His gaze traveled the length of her body, and her heart began to beat faster.

As she stood staring, knowing he wanted her to come to him, she needed to push him a little, to draw out the dom in him. She needed to see the stern look of his eyes as they met hers, needed to hear his deep, commanding voice. It excited her.

It turned her on.

She leaned casually against the kitchen table. "I thought you were hungry?" she asked. "Then why are you standing over there? Sit down and let's eat something."

His eyes narrowed, and his lips pursed as he looked at her, his arms coming to cross his chest as his gaze met hers. "Come here."

An instruction. An order, even. If she disobeyed him now, he might punish her.

Anticipation swirled in her belly, a pulse low in her gut as his eyes met hers. When she didn't immediately obey him, he cocked a brow then uncrossed his arms, his hands going to his hips, accentuating his bridled strength. His hands were large and strong, and her gaze followed upward, the length of his dark forearms to his thicker, muscled biceps stretched against the t-shirt that hugged his arms, the muscles pulling the fabric taut. Those were hands that had done wicked, violent things. He'd hurt people. He'd broken bones. She could see scrapes along his knuckles, and a few faint bruises. She wondered how he'd gotten them. Those were the hands, though…

He'd *spanked* her.

What else had he done? What else had he seen?

From where she stood, the heat of his gaze made warmth flood to her chest and cheeks as she slowly dragged her feet to him. He did not move but waited for her, his gaze calculating as she moved closer, within his grasp now, her heart pitter-pattering against her chest, heat flaring in her belly.

Were those the eyes of a man who'd taken lives? All for the greater good? Was she standing on the precipice of her future—falling for a man who didn't take no for an answer, but expected obedience? And as she drew closer, each passing second making her tremble, he reached for her, grasped her waist and yanked her between his legs.

He placed one hand on her lower back, pressing her against him, while the other went to her hair, first threading his fingers through it, combing it, the soft touch making her tremble, before slowly twirling his fist around the long blonde waves and tugging her head back.

Nora's mouth dropped open when he pulled, and his mouth met hers in a possessive, heated kiss that made her gasp, thankful he held her upright. Under his power, surrounded by his strength, she asked herself again, *Is this my future?*

God, she hoped so.

The self-doubt that plagued her made her wonder sometimes. Diego could be scary. He'd done wicked things he couldn't even talk about. Was she attracted to the danger? Did she find herself with a bad boy because that's all she'd ever seen in her childhood, her mother bringing home one outlaw after another? *Is this how I'm damaged?*

His mouth on hers, his hands in her hair and at her waist, she was his prisoner.

No, it didn't feel like damage. It felt right and she fucking loved it.

He took his mouth off hers just long enough to whisper in her ear, "You playing games with me, Norita?" He underscored his question with a sharp tug of her hair.

"No," she gasped, but another tug had her questioning her answer.

She shivered as his whiskers grazed her neck before his deep voice rumbled in her ear once more. "Are you lying to me, little girl? You know what happens to little girls who lie to their daddies."

She shook her head, needing just enough of his attention without wanting to actually push him over the edge and earn herself punishment.

"No, Daddy," she whispered. "I'm not lying."

"Oh?" he asked. Still grasping her hair, he tugged so that her neck lay bare before him. Lowering his mouth, he lapped at the sensitive skin by her collarbone before slowly grazing his teeth along her skin. "When I call you, Nora," he said, his voice deep, chiding. "You come to Daddy right away. Understood?"

"Yes, Daddy," she whispered, reveling in the way her the words made her feel safe and secure, yet aroused. He released her hair, and she dropped her head to his chest. His hand at her back snaked downward, cupping her ass and squeezing. She drew in a breath but did not protest, enjoying the possessive feel of his touch.

"Good," he said, his voice as deep, making her shiver. "Because if you didn't? Then Daddy would have to spank you." He gave her one sharp swat to demonstrate.

Her panties dampened between her thighs even as her heart tripped in anticipation. A spanking from Diego was no joke. But perhaps that was the point.

"Are you hungry, Nora?" he asked, his mouth back at her ear as he pulled the lobe between his lips and sucked. The touch of his tongue made her squirm.

She nodded, her stomach growling as if on cue. It'd been hours since she'd eaten, and even then, it hadn't been much. "Good, then."

He released her waist, and she gave a little mewl of protest, but he tugged her along with one hand, grabbing the food he'd purchased with the other, until they'd come to the master bedroom, his room, decorated in greens and blues, with simple, almost spartan furnishings.

He let go of her hand and pointed to the bed. "Sit up on the bed and kick off your shoes. Get comfy, honey. I'll get us something to drink."

She dropped her shoes on the floor and climbed up onto the bed, sitting back against the bunches of pillows. He came in the room, carrying a tray with a bottle of wine, two glasses, and sparkling water.

"Wine?" he asked.

"Sure," she shrugged. "But I'm more of a beer drinker."

He barked out a laugh, and slid the tray on the bedside table. "I hate wine. I drink whiskey or beer, but figured you, being the more refined one, would like wine."

She smiled at his honesty, and nodded. "I don't drink very often," she confessed, shrugging one shoulder. "I guess it's natural when your mom drinks alcohol like water."

He frowned. "Yeah," he said. "My parents' church didn't believe in drinking." He laughed mirthlessly. "But, the fact that I do drink would be the least of the sins I commit."

She didn't speak at first as he uncorked the bottle and poured the golden liquid into a wine glass, the smell of fermented grapes wafting in the room. He lifted it to his mouth and sipped, then grimaced. "God, this is shit."

Nora laughed out loud. "Then keep it and I'll use it to cook with."

He cocked a brow. "You cook?"

"Um, well. I can make about three things. But those three things are delicious. Even Tony likes them."

Tony, her sister's Tessa's husband, owned *Cara*, one of the most successful Italian restaurants in the North End. He had impeccable taste when it came to food. Just before Nora had graduated high school, Tony and Tessa had welcomed Nora into their apartment to live so she could escape her abusive mother, and Nora had come to accept Tony as her older brother.

"Eh, get the Angelico brothers hungry enough, they'll eat anything," he teased, lifting the glass to his lips and taking another sip. He grimaced, and she laughed.

"Hey," she said. "Works for me. Um, I'm taking it that you're not getting into the wine?"

"Swill," he said, putting the glass down on the table. "Want some?"

"You tell me it's swill and offer me some? Is that any way to woo a girl?" she teased, as he opened the sparkling water and poured it into the empty wine glass.

He looked at her out of the corner of her eye. "Honey, I don't need alcohol to woo *this* girl," he said.

She laughed out loud as he handed her the glass. "Is that so, Captain Confident?"

He placed a sandwich on her plate, and opened the bag of chips, placing a few beside the sandwich. "You'll see, *mija*," he said. He handed her the plate, and her stomach growled. She waited until he fixed his and sat up next to her in bed. "Eat, Nora," he said.

She lifted the sandwich and peeked at it. Looked like some sorta chicken Caesar salad wrap. Growing up with a mother who questioned every single thing she ate, Nora sometimes felt uncomfortable eating in front of other people, but she worked hard at being normal about it. "Okay," she said, watching him as he swallowed a large bite of his sandwich.

His eyes sobered and he swallowed. "When we're alone? That's yes, Daddy."

Her pulse spiked and she took a sip of water to swallow her nerves. "Yes, Daddy."

As they ate, he asked her about *Centered*, and Tessa, and how things were going with Tony and Tessa's little family. After she finished her sandwich and washed it down with a good amount of water, she felt better. Her focus was clearer now.

"Good girl," he said, taking her plate from her. She wasn't used to being served like this, and she wasn't quite sure how it made her feel. "You ready for dessert?" he asked.

"I'm full after that," she said. "I was actually thinking I could take a nap now." And just to accentuate her teasing, she closed her eyes and leaned back against the pillows. She *was* tired, but she was in no mood to rest.

"Diego!" she squealed, as seconds later he pounced, both hands at her wrists, holding them down on the bed while his mouth came to her ear.

"Take a nap?" he asked. "You little brat. I ought to spank your ass just for suggesting it." The threat, delivered in his deep baritone, traipsing along her skin like molten lava, made her moan out loud.

"Would you spank me, Daddy?" she asked.

"Damn right I would," he said. "You know better than that now, don't you?"

She grinned. "Yup."

"I think maybe I ought to wake you up," he whispered in her ear. "Maybe I should strip you, and take you across my knee. I should spank you until you scream for mercy. Redden that ass and teach you to obey your daddy."

"Mmmm," she moaned. "I'll be good, Daddy."

"I bought some berries and whipped cream," he said. "You stay right here." He released her wrists and, when he stood, he adjusted himself. She giggled and he only fixed with her a stern look as he leaned down, stretched her legs out and pressed her wrists into the bed. "You, young lady," he said. "Stay *right. There.*"

He got up and left the room and she heard him padding to the kitchen before he rummaged through the refrigerator. Her nose itched a bit but she dared not move, conscious of her wrists on his clean, cool sheets, her legs spread out on the bed, and as she lay there she became aware of the weight of her clothes on her body, the throbbing of her pussy, and her dry mouth. She closed her eyes and tipped her head to the side as she waited for him, her chest rising and falling with each breath she took and released.

"Good girl," she heard, his deep voice making her nipples

tighten and her tummy dip. She opened her eyes, and he stood in the doorway, leaning against it, watching her.

"Aren't you a sight for sore eyes," he said, eyeing her before pushing off the doorway and into the room, one side of his beautiful mouth quirking up as he prowled over to her, his bare feet noiselessly moving across the hardwood floor. "Did you stay there exactly like Daddy told you?" he asked.

She nodded. "Yes, Daddy. Of course I did."

"Ah. A very good girl," he said, coming over to the bed. He placed a bowl of berries next to her, and the can of whipped cream next to it. She eyed him, her heartbeat accelerating, her breath quickening. If this were anyone else, she'd laugh at him, thinking the whole whipped-cream-in-bed thing sounded trite or silly. But with Diego, there was no trite and definitely not silly.

His voice dropped, and the humor left his face. "Don't forget what Daddy told you," he said. "Stay right there. No matter what, baby, you don't move or I *will* take off my belt. Yeah?"

She swallowed hard and nodded. He would.

He gave one curt nod in reply. "Good girl." He knelt next to her and grasped the edge of her top, slowly lifting it and exposing a little strip of bare skin at her belly. His eyes heated and he dipped his face low, lapping at the bare skin with a slow, warm swipe of his tongue. She gasped, but kept her hands in position. His gaze met hers, his mouth so close to her sensual parts that the pounding of her heart beat harder, faster, and he slowly lifted her top even higher, exposing more skin.

He placed both hands on either side of her torso, kneeling on the bed, letting the scruff of his beard scrape along her naked skin. "So beautiful," he said, raising her top high enough to expose her bra. "Lift your hands, baby," he said. She arched her back, and he took her top off. He tossed it to the floor, where it crumpled in a heap, and when he came back, he began to unfasten the front clasp of her bra. Her breath became labored and choppy, and her chest rose and fell as she fought to keep her position. With a snap, her bra came undone, and her breasts spilled free as he took her in with greedy eyes. "Christ," he said in a low voice, cupping her breasts and puckering her nipples with the pad of his thumb. He swallowed hard, and suddenly, she felt *beautiful*.

"Stay there, honey," he said, grabbing the can of whipped cream and giving it a shake before tearing the top off. "You like whipped cream?" he asked. She giggled.

"Um, yes, Daddy," she said.

"Excellent," he said. He knelt on the bed, leaned over and painted her naked breasts with the whipped cream. She gasped from the cold, but didn't move as he lowered his body on hers and lapped at the cream, pulling one nipple wholly into his mouth and sucking.

"Oh my God," she said, her hips jerking, and then he went to the next nipple and licked her clean, pulling her nipple into his mouth a second time.

"Ah, good girl," he said. "Got a little worried there. Thought I'd have to spank you."

She shook her head from side to side. "No, Daddy," she choked. "I'll be good." He grinned, pushing off the bed and grabbing the bowl of berries. He took one and popped it into his mouth, then swallowed as she watched him with rapt attention.

"Want one, baby?" he asked. She nodded. Kneeling on the bed, he leaned over and dangled a plump berry over her mouth. "Say please," he said, shaking his head from side to side. "Only polite little girls get what they want."

"Please?" she asked and his eyes narrowed, as he shook his head from side to side. "Please, Daddy?" she amended, and he grinned. He placed the strawberry in her mouth. It burst with tart sweetness as she chewed and swallowed.

"Good girl," he said. "Open up." She did, and he squirted whipped cream in her mouth, then seconds later, his mouth came to hers and he sucked on her lower lip, licking the cream off her mouth. "So sweet," he mumbled. "Delicious." His tongue plundered hers as he straddled her, lowering his body against hers and grinding against her, his rock hard erection between her legs, and even with him fully clothed, she felt her need rising.

He pulled back and smiled at her. "You're such a good girl," he said. "You can move your hands now, baby. I want to do you soft and sweet tonight." Her hands wrapped around his broad neck as his mouth met hers, a soft, sensual kiss she felt all the way down to her toes. "That's my girl," he said. "Such a very good girl." Releasing her, he pushed away. "Now strip for me, baby." She fumbled with the zipper of her skirt, then shimmied it down her legs. He grabbed the fabric at her ankles, freed her legs, and tossed the skirt to the floor. "Panties off," he ordered next, raising his brows as he nodded to the panties as if they were a major inconvenience and he needed them to go, *now*, before he started knocking skulls together.

She obeyed, hands shaking as she took them off.

"God," he said, his eyes going half-lidded, his voice low and heated as he came back to her. "You're a fucking dream come true," he said. He nudged her knees apart with his and kissed her again, on her temple and then the bridge of her nose, followed by her lips and then her neck, trailing kisses along her collarbone and down to her breasts.

"Open up, baby," he said, moving her knees open. "Are you ready?"

Ready? She was about to come if he so much as *breathed* on her again.

"Yes," she croaked. "Yes, Daddy!" Watching him unfasten his jeans, she shivered, as his bare skin glistened in the dim light of the open door. He was lean and muscled, his body controlled and powerful. Bending down to her, he kissed her once more, nudging her knees further apart, then he lowered his mouth to her ear.

"Sweetest thing I've ever seen," he murmured, as he drew

closer, his skin meeting hers, warm and electric as they connected. "I wanna make love to you, Nora. And I want you to remember this." His broad shoulders lowered as his arms encircled her, the silky head of his cock at her entrance as she held onto him, the firm muscles at his neck and back strong and masculine, his arms tight around her. He was everything she fought and everything she needed. She could see it in the way he looked at her, the possessive heat of his eyes and firm touch of his hand, his arm around her shoulders and voice at her ear. He loved her.

With one firm push, he entered her. She gasped, holding onto his shoulders for support, a thrill of ecstasy threading through her core with every move of his hips. "You're mine, Nora," he said, the warmth of his breath at her ear while he slid in, making her quake beneath him. She didn't want to be anyone's but his, *ever*. She only wanted Diego, every bossy, sweet inch of him. And as he moved, slowly building a rhythm, she wanted to be what he needed… the strong woman who could take him, who would understand even the deepest, darkest part of his soul, so she could love him better. She wanted to heal him of his broken past, help him be the man he longed to become, get to know the man he already was. He was a man who'd sacrificed himself to protect the innocents, a man who'd faced darkness others couldn't handle.

He held her, their bodies moving as one, her pleasure building with every thrust of his hips. His forehead met hers in a silent understanding as she gripped onto him. She was going to lose control, and so was he. His breathing became choppy, her own breath caught in her throat, somewhere between ecstasy and need. When she finally hit the cusp of pleasure, they came together, a fusion of perfection. They held each other in the dim light of dusk, his forehead still against hers.

They lay in the darkness, and she shifted her position slightly so her head could rest on his chest. They didn't say anything. Her fingers entwined with his and they rested in the quiet, sheets tossed haphazardly over them. The little prickly hairs on his chest tickled her cheek, and the warmth of his skin against hers gave her comfort. It felt nice, lying here with him. It felt right.

"You okay, baby?" he asked, a quiet question that meant so much. He'd just made sweet love to her, and brought pleasure only he could bring. But it wasn't about the sex. His question ran deeper than that.

Was she okay?

She needed one helluva chat with her big sister. It would be good to see Diego with the others again, with the friends who'd come to be her family and his. A small part of her wanted their blessing, but she realized as he held her in his bed that the woman in her needed no one's approval.

"Yeah," she said softly, her voice barely audible. "I'm... more than okay." She paused before asking what she needed to know. "Are you?"

She heard him swallow hard before bringing her fingers to his mouth and kissing them. "Yeah, baby," he said. "I am now."

Chapter 7

"The intel is good, and the plan is solid," Diego told the man on the other side of his desk.

Tomás leaned back in his chair and propped his feet up on the wooden surface between them. "But?"

Diego ignored the muddy boots parked inches from his face and purposely hesitated for a moment before replying, "But something about this seems off to me."

Tomás fished a pack of cigarettes from his shirt pocket and lit one, while the gaze he fixed on Diego danced with amusement. "Padre, it's a five minute in and out. Spot the girl, squeeze the trigger, run like hell. Easy as fuck."

Diego inhaled a smoke-laden breath, and reminded himself to keep his temper in check. Tomás's disrespect and contempt for Diego's authority wore on his nerves, and he had to fight the urge to put the man in his place. *This is what needs to happen now,* he reminded himself. *You need to appear just weak and hesitant enough for him to doubt you. Let Tomás's own arrogance bring him down so you can protect Nora, Camila, and the other girls.*

Diego nodded at Tomás and allowed a thread of nervousness to enter his voice. "Yeah. Right. Easy as fuck."

Tomás rolled his eyes. "*Jesus*. Listen to you. My five-year-old niece has more *cojones* than you do right now. You're gonna punk out, aren't you?"

Jackpot. I should win an Oscar for this.

Diego narrowed his own eyes and played the part he'd written for himself, stammering, "What? No. Fuck you. Why would you think that? I said I'd take the girl out tomorrow night, and I will. I just said it seems... *off.*"

"Padre, *everything's* been off with you this week... Even longer, if I'm being honest." The man arched his back and stretched, making himself comfortable in Diego's chair, in Diego's space.

"What's that supposed to mean?" Diego demanded.

"*Pfft.* You know. Going easy on Ricky." Tomás flicked the ash of his cigarette onto the floor and watched Diego thoughtfully. "Not having us all out there immediately searching for the girl." He pursed his lips. "Hardly a secret that you've lost your mojo. All the guys are talking about it. You don't have the heart for this anymore, let alone the balls."

Diego stared back, hard and cool, but inside, his chest twisted in wry acknowledgement. Tomás was half right—Diego hadn't had the heart for this job for a long time, if ever. But he had the balls to admit he'd deluded himself into thinking that being one of the "good guys" excused the crimes he'd had to commit to protect his identity, even as he'd felt his soul blackening by the day. He regretted the deception he was employing on Tomás, regretted that it had come to this, but he didn't want anyone else harmed for the sake of the investigation. The lies he told would save Camila's life.

"*All* the guys have been talking about it?" Diego repeated, as though he didn't know it to be true. "Including you?"

Tomás shrugged and smiled offhandedly. "You and me, we go back a long time, Padre, but you know how it is around here. One of your boys starts to lose his nerve, it makes you wonder... How long until he turns on the crew? How long until he gets *my* ass killed? How long until he's a liability?" He sucked in a deep drag from the cigarette before adding, "Ain't personal."

Diego snorted, ostensibly at Tomás's *ain't personal* line, because both of them knew without a shadow of a doubt that this was very personal indeed, but also because of the irony in Tomás's earlier words. *How long until Diego turned?* Ha. Diego had turned on them almost from the very beginning.

"I am *not* a liability," Diego told the other man, reciting the line Tomás would expect from him while allowing his very real anger at the whole fucked up situation to come through in his voice. "And the only person who's gonna get you killed is *you*, coming into my office and talking out your ass like this!"

Tomás took another drag from the cigarette and inspected the lit tip, patently unafraid. "I'm just expressing my concerns." He turned his gaze on Diego again. "It's an easy job for tomorrow, but I'd feel more confident about your ability to get this handled if I knew your plan and the girl's location ahead of time. Remember, the other day you agreed to share information with me."

"And I did. I told you the basic plan."

"And I told *you*, that's not good enough, Padre," Tomás interrupted. "Not anymore. I want the girl's address. I want the details."

Diego clenched his teeth, a picture of reluctance.

"*Now*, Padre," Tomás demanded.

"Fine." Diego huffed out a breath. He grabbed his phone, unlocked it, and typed out a quick message—a dummy address far from Lucas and Grace's townhouse that he and Slay had devised the day before. A second later, Tomás's phone dinged as the message arrived.

"That's the address my contact gave me for the foster home where the girl is staying," Diego told him. "I cased the place yesterday. There's a stand of trees on one side of the house with a clear view of the front walk, and I'll wait there. House is pretty well secured. Hard to gain entry. Gotta get her in transit. Her schedule is pretty varied, but my contact assured me she had some follow-up meeting with a social worker at the house at six o'clock Friday night. That's when I'll take care of things. In plenty of time to meet El Jefe's deadline."

"Tomorrow there'll be one day left before the deadline. That isn't plenty of time," Tomás argued.

"It's enough."

Tomás nodded slowly. "If you say so. I assume you have a backup plan?"

Diego let his face flush angrily. "What, you're analyzing *every* decision I make now? Want me to alert you next time I need to take a piss? Remember who's in charge here, Tomás."

Tomás held his gaze and waited.

When Diego felt he'd stalled long enough to sell the lie, he continued grudgingly, "Big yellow house across the street two doors down is empty and has a clear view of the room where the girl is staying. I can go there after dark and take the shot if the first location isn't viable."

He saw a considering light appear in Tomás's eyes.

Diego leaned forward and shoved the other man's boots towards the edge of the desk, making it clear that his temper had been pushed too far. "And when this is done, Tomás? When I have taken care of the girl and saved our asses from El Jefe? You and I are going to have a reckoning. I'm going to make sure El Jefe knows about your insolence, and we'll see how he suggests dealing with you."

Tomás smiled bitterly. "Oh, we'll see all right, Padre. When El Jefe finds out, you'll wish you had taken my advice the other day."

Diego glared, jaw locked. His anger was real and visible, but it wasn't *just* anger riding him. Tomás was cocksure, bold, and oh-so-fucking-young, just like the rest of the crew. Even now, even knowing how easily Tomás had suggested killing Ricky and how sanguine all the guys had been about sanctioning the death of an innocent teenager like Camila, there was something inside Diego that wanted to protect the man. Years of camaraderie, sharing good memories and bad over bottles of tequila and *aguardiente*, were impossible for his heart to overlook, even as his head reminded him of his ultimate goal. Part of him wanted to save Tomás and *all* the guys from their own stupidity and bad choices…

The way you couldn't save Armando?

Grief he'd buried for years stabbed through his chest and he looked away from Tomás. His little brother had been that young and cocky once, relishing the idea of challenging authority and living life on his own terms. He'd believed signing up with Chalo Salazar would bring him respect and wealth, never dreaming that he'd be left to bleed out in the middle of Meridian Street on a cold, January night while Diego did Salazar's dirty work in another part of town.

Better Tomás ends up in jail than dead when you're not around to protect him, he reminded himself. *In betraying him this way, you'll be saving his life.*

Even so, he couldn't stop himself from warning once more, "I still have a bad feeling. Maybe we could postpone…"

He was almost hoping, despite everything, that Tomás would hear the warning in his words, that he wouldn't take the bait… that he *wouldn't* attempt to cut Diego out by killing the girl himself *tonight*.

That hope died the moment Tomás's boots hit the floor with a resounding *thud* and he pushed himself to his feet with a smile. "Calm yourself, Padre. Everything's under control," he said as he walked towards the door. "Just don't lose your nerve. Stick to the plan."

Diego smiled grimly and slid out his phone to send another text, this one to Slay. *Op is in motion. He's taking the bait.*

He would stick to the plan, for all their sakes.

DIEGO SAT STRAIGHT up in bed, gasping, and his head swiveled toward each shadowed corner of the room in turn, instinctively searching for threats.

Nothing. The only sound besides the frantic pounding of his heart was the quiet, steady breathing of the woman in bed next to him. *Nora. Safe and sound.*

He sucked in a deep breath and pushed a hand through his long hair, noting that it was actually damp with sweat despite the chill in the air. Remnants of fear and anguish clawed at his chest. He couldn't remember exactly what he'd been dreaming about—some crazy mash-up of Armando's death, his betrayal of Tomás, and all the other sins on his conscience that would never fully be forgiven. He couldn't believe he'd managed to fall asleep tonight at all.

He reached for the phone on the nightstand and saw that it was just after midnight. Had Tomás taken the bait Diego had laid out? Had he made a play for the girl? Had he been apprehended? There was no update from Slay.

"Everything okay, Daddy?" came a sleepy voice from beside him.

He swallowed, forcing his voice to be calm and reassuring. "Yeah, baby. Everything's fine." He laid back down and wrapped his arm around her, pulling her so her head was pillowed on his shoulder.

She burrowed against him with a contented murmur and lifted her hand to caress his cheek. A moment later, he could feel her eyes pop open as she felt his sweat-dampened skin.

"Diego? Are you sick? Is something wrong?"

"Nah. It's just stuffy in here," he lied. "I'm fine. Back to sleep, babe."

"Bad dream?" she murmured.

He could feel his body tense beneath her. "What makes you ask that?"

She shrugged. "Sometimes you twitch and moan when you're sleeping. Like you're trying to fight someone, or someone's fighting *you*."

"Or maybe I'm trying to hold you across my lap in my dream," he teased, hoping she couldn't hear that his heart had picked up its pace again. This was another reason why he hadn't shared a bed with anyone in years. He didn't want to know what sorts of things he might have said in his sleep. He fought his demons at night—the one's he couldn't fully face in the daylight. "Maybe I'm sleep-spanking you."

She giggled. "You dream of spanking me? Why does this not surprise me?" But instead of burrowing in again, she braced her arm against his chest and lifted her head to stare down at him. "Want to talk about anything? Earlier tonight, you seemed kind of distracted."

He felt himself smiling in the darkness at her willingness to provide comfort even in the middle of the night. "Nothing to talk about," he said softly.

More like, nothing he *would* talk about. He wouldn't burden her with the knowledge that he'd set up one of his top lieutenants to be arrested tonight, or that he was still fucking conflicted about it even though he knew it was necessary. He wouldn't express his increasing suspicions about Diana Consuelos, the woman Nora considered her mentor. And he definitely wouldn't tell her how unreasonably annoyed he was that Slay, while agreeing to investigate Diana, refused to bar the woman from *Centered* while the investigation was pending based solely on Diego's gut feeling.

"Diego, man, I'm looking into her. I have Heidi and Paul going over her finances with a fine-toothed comb, and they're working fast," Slay had said when Diego had called for a status update earlier in the evening. "But Diana's a big-ticket donor who's promised a huge check Saturday night. I can't tell Elena that I'm kicking the woman out on her ass—and potentially losing a donation that could save the lives of dozens of women—on the basis of your suspicions."

On paper, Slay was right, and Diego knew it. There was zero hard evidence tying Diana to any criminal activity. His friends Heidi Angelico and her business partner Paul Lozano, a dominant who often visited The Club with his boyfriend John, were widely regarded as the best financial analysts and forensic accountants in the business, so Diego knew they'd uncover any scrap of evidence there was to be found. He should be able to wait it out, be patient and logical.

But Diego's gut instinct had been honed for situations just like this—situations where recognizing the difference between a coincidence and a red flag could mean the difference between life and death—and it was pissing him off that no one else seemed to be taking the danger seriously.

No, he wasn't going to tell Nora any of that, either.

"Nothing to say," he continued, pulling her down against his chest once more. "Besides, I'm not sure I appreciate the suggestion that I was distracted earlier. Did you not feel that I gave you *one hundred percent* of my attention?"

She smirked until he reached a hand beneath the sheet and caressed her naked ass, causing her to squirm.

"N-no, Daddy, I definitely felt *that*," she breathed, and he grinned.

Earlier that night, he'd spanked her—not hard, since there was no punishment involved, but just enough to remind her that he was in charge and that she'd agreed to submit to his authority. It had been incredibly arousing for them both and had helped him to quiet his own worries about keeping her safe, at least temporarily.

"Good," he said firmly. "I need to make sure you never forget that I'm your daddy. That I'll take care of you and keep you safe, no matter what." He traced patterns along the smooth skin of her back, and he allowed himself to breathe in the perfection of that moment.

She swallowed hard. "You know… I'm a pretty lucky girl."

He blinked down at her in the darkness. Between her self-centered bitch of a mother and the shit she'd been forced to endure as a child, Diego didn't generally think of Nora as lucky. "I think it's strength more than luck," he told her. "Not one woman in a thousand could live through what you've lived through and still be the loving, generous person you are."

He could feel her smile against his chest, and it thrilled him. But then she shook her head. "See, that's what I mean, though. It *was* shitty. But, I've had people looking out for me along the way. Tess and Tony, who pretty much became my parents after I moved out of my mom's. Slay, who took a bullet for me when you guys rescued me from Roger. Elena and Allie, who've always reminded me of the gifts I have to offer the world. And you…"

"Me?" he repeated.

"Mm-hmm. Looking out for me, like my personal guardian angel, even when I didn't want you to be, and coming back into my life to be my daddy when I didn't know I needed it."

He pressed his lips to her forehead. "That makes you feel lucky?"

"Of course. Recently, that's the thing I'm *most* thankful for," she said simply, as though the words weren't bittersweet barbs that landed in his heart. Then she went on, "Oh, and I'm super lucky to have *Centered*. I know I've talked about it a billion times, but I love working there, knowing I'm making a difference."

"That's important," Diego agreed. "Sometimes knowing you're making a difference is the most important thing."

"Oh, and there's Diana," Nora said. "God, I'm so lucky to have that woman in my life."

Diego sucked in a breath and felt tension coil in his body. He knew Nora felt it too when she sighed. "We're not going to start this again, are we? This thing where you tell me I need to be suspicious of everyone's motives, and I remind you that Diana is a good person who's only ever helped me?"

It was on the tip of Diego's tongue to open up to her, to tell her all about the pending investigation, but he knew that, without proof, Nora would tell him he was crazy and utterly wrong. He sent up a quick prayer that Heidi and Paul finished their financial analysis ASAP, and that Nora would let the matter drop.

"No," he gritted out. "We don't need to discuss it."

"Good," Nora said softly. "Because Diana suggested something to me today, and I almost didn't want to tell you about it because I thought you might overreact. You have to..." She paused, then rephrased, "I mean, I would *like it* if you would *please*... listen to the whole thing before you say anything, Daddy."

"I'm listening," he told her, mentally vowing that no matter what she told him, he would do his best not to speak before thinking through his response.

He felt Nora's tongue sneak out to wet her lips, inadvertently touching his chest in the process. His cock stirred to life, distracting him from his good intentions.

"Nora," he gritted out. "Spill."

"Well... Diana sat down with me earlier today and we chatted about my future. Sort of a 'where do you see yourself in five or ten years?' kind of thing. She says she sees loads of potential in me. She was really pleased with the job I did on the fundraiser, and how I've really helped *Centered* grow from a small, local clinic to a shelter and outreach center for women and children around Boston."

"Right." He commended himself on his even tone. He did not like the woman and there was no other reason for it than his instincts.

Nora pushed up further and he could feel her stare through the darkness. She took a deep breath, then said in an excited rush, "Turns out she has a position in her company for someone young and bright, like me. She wants me to be her communications director. I'd be doing a million different things—which is exactly what I like, having all that variety! I'd be working with the charities she endows, doing some fundraising, plus making some determinations about new charities to fund. I'd be able to have a huge, global impact, far beyond what I'm able to do at *Centered*. A broader platform! And the best part is, the job is in Miami! *Miami*, Diego! You could leave your undercover work and…"

Her words were still coming out at a mile a minute, but at a certain point he'd stopped listening. "She offered you a job?" he interrupted, setting his broad palm against her cheek.

Nora stacked her hands on his chest and rested her chin on them. "Well, basically, yes. There's an opening and she could fast-track the interview process, make it just a formality. And, well, I mean, I know it's early for us to really be thinking about the future…" He could feel her hot blush against his hand. "But maybe starting over together would be a good thing."

"Nora… you…" His gut was churning. "You can*not* go to work for Diana."

So much for that vow to think before speaking.

He felt, more than saw, her eyes narrow. "Daddy… Diego… there are some things you can tell me to do and I'll do them, but… You can't just lay down the law about something like this. We have to *discuss* it, don't we? I get a say in my own life."

Her voice sounded so hesitant, and he wanted to reassure her, to tell her that *yes, of course*, that's exactly how things *should* work, but he couldn't. His heart was beating in his throat, and he could only imagine the worst-case scenarios—a sick, twisted asshole like El Jefe gaining even closer access to his woman, and Nora somehow injured or killed as a result. Instinctive, absolute denial roared in his chest.

"No, Nora, that's *not* how this works," he told her flatly. "You can't make a decision about this when you don't have all the facts."

"All the facts?" she cried, pushing off his chest to sit up straight. "You're saying *I* don't have all the facts? You've never even *met* Diana, but you've decided that you don't like her because... *why*? Because it's weird to you that a rich woman would want to help other women? Because she gives me time and attention, and reminds me that I can do bigger and better things than I'm doing right now? Because you go through life thinking every single person is a serial killer who's out to get you, and you want me to become paranoid like you? God!"

She swung her legs over the edge of the bed. A moment later, the soft, yellow light of the lamp on her nightstand filled the room.

"Enough!" Diego said, leaning up on one elbow. He could hear the fury vibrating in his own voice and fought to temper it. "That's *more* than enough. It's the middle of the night, Nora. Get your ass back into bed and we can discuss this like reasonable people in the morning."

But Nora shook her head and began pacing the room in her sleeveless nightshirt, her arms wrapped around herself. "No, we'll do this *now*. Diana is an amazing person, and if you just gave her a shot..."

Diego sat up, bracing his back against the headboard, and pressed the heels of his hands against his eyes. He wanted to order her back to bed, to force her to abandon this whole conversation until he had the evidence he needed. If he insisted, reminded her that he was her daddy, he knew she'd do it. But one look at her eyes—wide, questioning, *hurting*—had him reversing his position. This relationship would never be about what was easiest or most convenient for *him*, but about giving her what she needed, even when it was hard.

"I'm sure she *seems* like a lovely person, but appearances can be deceiving," he said. "I just want you to be cautious, little girl."

"Daddy, you don't get it! Diana sees my potential, she tells me I'm talented and capable. She believes in me! My whole life, I've wanted someone to see me that way!"

He met her angry brown eyes with his own. "Tess sees you that way," he growled. "Elena does, Alice does. And I do, too."

But she was shaking her head even before he finished speaking. "I know, but that's different! Diana's older. She's like… she's like…"

"Like the mom you wished you had?"

Her shoulders slumped. "Maybe, yeah." And then, a second later, more loudly, "Yeah, *exactly* like that! My own mom did nothing but tell me what a failure I was, and how I'd never amount to anything. Diana wants to give me opportunities, to help me share my ideas on a broader platform so I can help more people! What's so wrong with that? Why can't you be happy for me?"

Diego shook his head. Despite the hero-worship in Nora's voice when she talked about Diana, Diego hadn't realized just how far the woman's power over Nora extended. Nora's heart was going to be shattered when she learned the truth. It made his anger towards Diana kick up a notch, even as his sympathy for his girl swelled.

"Ah, *mamita*. There's nothing wrong with wanting someone to be your mentor or your champion, but you're letting it blind you! You don't know anything about this woman's background. You can't be sure of her true motives. You have no idea what she's done…"

"Like *you*?" Nora's eyes were blazing with accusation. "I don't know anything about what you've done either, *Diego*, but I'm supposed to trust *you*, right? How many people who've trusted you have wished *they* had been more cautious?"

Pain lanced through his chest. In a flash, he swung his legs off the bed and faced her. "I have never lied to you, Nora. There are things I don't tell you because I don't want to upset you, and

I don't want you to worry. And, yeah, there are things I don't tell you because I'm fucking ashamed of them. I have *never* claimed to have lived a blameless life. *Christ.* But when I tell you something? When I tell you that I believe in you, that you are incredibly intelligent, that I am in awe of the way you connect with people and the selfless way you care for them? You'd better believe that I mean every fucking word."

Her shoulders slumped, and she looked smaller and more fragile than Diego had ever seen her. He held out his arms to her.

She looked at him, at his arms, longingly, but shook her head. "Right here and right now, Daddy," she whispered. "You tell me I can trust you, that you've never lied to me, *so right here and now* tell me… What do you have against Diana?"

Fuck. He had not wanted it to come to this tonight. She'd never believe him, that much was clear from her tirade. And how could he protect her if she didn't? He studied her for a moment —her raised chin, her determined eyes. His woman, his babygirl. *His Nora.*

Diego pushed his hair back from his face with both hands and began. "We've been trying to apprehend the leader of a sex trafficking ring, a man… or rather, a *person*… known only as El Jefe."

"The Boss?" Nora translated.

"Exactly." Nora took a seat on the edge of the bed, while Diego began to pace. "This person is careful to never show their face on camera. All interaction is done via text and calls from burner cell phones, and El Jefe always uses a voice changer. Nobody knows what El Jefe looks like or what they sound like. Physically, we've got nothing."

He glanced at Nora who was watching him attentively. "We've worked extensively with law enforcement—both local and national—to come up with a profile of this person. They're ruthless, narcissistic, and accustomed to being in charge," he ticked the items off on his fingers. "And this person has business interests—likely legitimate interests—in Boston and Miami, since those are El Jefe's two power bases."

He saw comprehension begin to dawn in Nora's eyes. "And you think…"

"I have spoken to El Jefe several times," he interrupted. "I don't know the exact tone of their voice, thanks to the voice changer, but there are some things that can't be hidden—cadence, speech patterns, vocabulary. We know that El Jefe is a fluent Spanish speaker who uses specific phrases often. I have personally heard Diana Consuelos use the same cadence, the same phrases. She's a Spanish speaker. And both El Jefe and Diana have an assistant named Miguel."

He watched her carefully, saw her shaking her head in disbelief, and plowed on. "I asked Slay to investigate Diana, and he's having Heidi and Paul audit her financials. It's not enough for a warrant. It's all circumstantial evidence. But my gut instincts tell me that there's something there. And my instincts have saved my life too many times for me to ignore them now."

Nora swallowed hugged herself more tightly. "Is that it?"

Diego moved to sit next to her on the bed. "Yeah, baby. That's it. I have no proof that she's involved. But I don't want you to have anything to do with her until I can prove to my satisfaction that she's *not*."

Slowly, carefully, Nora nodded again, and when her eyes lifted to his, they were filled with tears. "Daddy… I have no idea what to believe here. If you knew Diana, you'd know how impossible that all is."

He sucked in a breath. She hadn't denied it outright. She'd called him *daddy*. Diego reached down and cupped her chin in his hand, forcing her to meet his eyes. "It comes down to this, Nora… Do you trust me to keep you safe?"

She bit her lip, hesitating. "Yes," she whispered. "I trust you, Daddy."

"All right, then," he told her, wrapping his arms around her and pulling her firmly against him. "That's where we start."

He tucked them both back into bed, cuddling Nora against his chest. She clung to him more tightly than before. It was a knife to his gut knowing that she was hurting because of the information he'd been forced to share, and that he couldn't take that pain away.

He smoothed his hand up and down her back, and as he felt her slowly relax into sleep, he whispered, "You think Diana will give you a chance to change the world. But I'm telling you, honey, you're already doing it. You changed Camila's life. You've changed mine."

DIEGO HAD JUST WATCHED the blackness outside the bedroom window fade to the murky, gray beginnings of dawn when his phone finally rang. He'd put it on silent hours before, just after Nora had fallen asleep, and had instead kept vigil, waiting for the device in his hand to light up with a call or a text from Slay, an update on the trap they'd constructed to apprehend Tomás.

Now the call had come, but from a number he didn't recognize. His heartbeat kicked up. He eased Nora onto her back and slid out of the bed, grabbing his t-shirt and jeans from the chair where he'd thrown them the night before and slipping out into the hallway before answering the call.

"Talk to me," he demanded, striding down to the living room. However, the voice that greeted him wasn't Slay's deep timbre, but a high, robotic one.

"Have you been waiting for my call, Padre?"

El Jefe was calling him? *Jesus*. Diego sank onto the sofa, swallowing hard. "Was I supposed to be, Jefe?"

El Jefe laughed. "You're the boss of my Boston operation, are you not? The man I tasked with making sure that a certain, er, *misplaced shipment* was handled appropriately?"

Diego's hand clenched into a fist against his knee and his grip on the phone tightened. "Of course."

"Then I can only assume you authorized the operation last night where Tomás Gutierrez shot a high-powered sniper rifle through the window of a supposed safe house in Wilmington? The operation where Tomás missed his intended target, if she was ever there to begin with, and was apprehended by the authorities?"

Oh God. El Jefe's people had learned the outcome of the plan to nab Tomás before Diego himself did! His heart nearly beat out of his chest. *Jefe was always going to learn about this eventually*, he reminded himself. *Later today, when Tomás was indicted. This is just faster than you expected. Play it cool.*

"No. I didn't authorize any operation last night," Diego said roughly. "My contact at *Centered* provided me with the address, assured me it was accurate. I told Tomás that I planned to hit the target there *tonight*. Myself."

"Ah, so your man went rogue." The voice was smug.

"Tomás is single-minded and hot-tempered," Diego hedged. "He probably thought he was doing the crew a favor. If and when he's released on bail, I'll make sure he's properly punished." *He'll be punished by a court of law*, he reminded himself with some satisfaction. *Not by my hand.* The plan had been for Slay's guys to catch Tomás in the act, so they would have enough evidence to make sure the man was denied bail, and Slay had promised to pass a message to his friend in the police department to make sure Tomás was put into protective custody immediately.

Which reminded him… where the hell *was* Slay? Why hadn't Slay called with this update himself?

"No need to worry about that," El Jefe said dismissively. "I've resolved that situation. But the matter of the girl remains. You have one more day, Padre."

Diego blinked. *Resolved?* His gut clenched as he forced himself to ask. "Resolved, Jefe? How so?"

A sigh, shrill and reedy. "In the usual way, Padre. The *permanent* way. I called in a favor and made sure he never made it out of his holding cell. Once a man goes rogue, it's only a matter of time before he turns on his crew, you know. And the last thing we need is *two* people running around knowing your crimes and your description. Isn't that right?"

No. He wanted to scream it aloud, to throw the phone against the fireplace and watch it shatter, obliterating El Jefe's words and making them untrue. Tomás dead? Murdered? He couldn't fit the words together, couldn't make sense of them. He'd wanted to *save* Tomás, but instead Diego's plan had condemned him.

Nora's words rang in his head. *How many people who trusted you wished they'd been more cautious?*

"Padre, I'm very busy." The tinny voice sounded bored... fucking *bored*, like the subject of Tomás's death was just one tiny blip on El Jefe's daily agenda. And though Tomás hadn't been a good man by anyone's definition, Diego mentally added him to the roster of people for whom he would seek retribution against El Jefe. *I will find you. I will make you bleed,* he vowed.

"Sorry, Jefe," Diego spat. "I was... surprised."

"Hmm. The way I see it, I rid you of a challenge to your authority. That means you owe me a favor."

The oily hatred that had been roiling in his stomach spread out each of his limbs like cold fire and he nearly choked as he replied, "That's one way to look at it."

El Jefe laughed, high and clear, and he remembered Diana's laugh from the other day. *You sick bitch.*

"You do amuse me, Padre! I suppose that's why I've kept you around as long as I have. But my amusement has reached its limit."

Diego sucked in a breath, pushing back the bile that threatened to rise to his throat, and proceeded with the plan he and

Slay had laid out. "I'll need more time. If the police identified Tomás, they'll know his associates. When the girl is killed, the first people they'll look for are…"

"One. Day. This is not flexible, not negotiable."

"But, Jefe…"

"Take care of this, Padre. Clean up your mess by tomorrow night. Or I promise you," the voice threatened. "I will clean it up for you."

Chapter 8

Nora studied herself in Diego's bathroom mirror, frowning. She clicked open her cosmetics bag and removed her concealer, twisted it open, then dabbed little dots under her eyes to mask the dark circles. She smoothed the make-up over with the pad of her middle finger, then applied a light layer of foundation and a touch of powder before running a mascara brush through her lashes. She forced a smile that didn't quite reach her eyes, so she could see if her handiwork helped. She looked pretty enough, she guessed, as she'd dolled herself up for the fundraiser. Since it was outside, she'd donned simple jeans and a white top, but done up her makeup and jewelry. But no, even the bottled beauty could not hide her fatigue and sadness.

More than a day after Diego's midnight revelations, things still weren't right between them. Nora had almost returned home the night before, but Diego's warnings about Diana had been worrying enough to keep Nora in his bed. In her head she told herself that it was a patently false accusation, that Diego was *trained* to see the evil in people, *trained* to suspect their motives, and he'd see evil lurking in the most innocent of places. For crying out loud, he practically did a background check on the guy who served her coffee at Dunkin Donuts before he let her take a sip. But he'd seen a lot, more than anyone should ever see, and his fears about Diana troubled Nora. His instincts had kept him alive.

Had the somewhat aloof glance Diana gave her the day before only been in Nora's mind, or was it related to something else? The way Diana had blinked dispassionately at the news that no one could locate their former clients, the women Diana herself had relocated to Miami, made Nora's belly churn.

No, she told herself. It couldn't be. How could the very woman who'd poured blood, sweat, and tears into the shelter, who brought light and love to so many actually be the one *responsible* for orchestrating an insidious crime ring? It was a false accusation. It *had* to be.

Fear wasn't the only thing that had kept her at Diego's house. Going home to her own place alone no longer appealed. Sleeping in her own cold bed paled in comparison to sleeping with the warmth and protection of Diego at her back, and she wanted that connection with him especially now, when things between them felt unresolved. Despite staying at his place, though, she'd hardly seen him since their argument, and spent her time as she worried and waited cleaning every inch of his house to keep her mind and hands occupied. He'd stayed out so late the night before, he'd climbed under the sheets beside her after she'd been asleep for hours, and when she'd woken this morning, he'd already started getting ready to go out again to who-knows-where. Though he'd kept tabs on her, checking in throughout the day with texts and phone calls, they hadn't so much as kissed.

Nora slammed her make-up bag on the counter and stared at her reflection, then drew a brush through her long, blonde hair. Diego liked it down, just so he could tug it when he wanted to. With a scowl, Nora fastened it into a bun at the nape of her neck, looped gold hoops through her ears, sighed, and left the bathroom.

Diego sat at the small kitchen table that overlooked the backyard. "Morning, beautiful," he said, sipping his coffee. "You about ready to go?"

"Yeah," she said, turning away from him. "I thought you'd have already left for work by now." She tried to keep the sting out of her tone, but wasn't successful.

He took another sip of coffee, then looked over at her from across the room before putting the mug down. His voice was sharp when he spoke. "Nice to see you, too, Nora." A pause, then, "Come here."

Despite her hidden anger, the deep timbre of his voice sent a shiver down her spine. She swallowed and stayed put.

"Do you really want to start the day like this, little girl?" he queried with a quirked brow, and she knew he expected—no, *demanded*—her obedience.

Did she want to begin the day like this? Too much warred within her. She wanted to hate him, to smack her hands against his unyielding chest, to rail against him for making her question someone who'd become such a fixture in her life and promised her opportunities she might never otherwise have. She wanted to scream that she'd worked too hard for her independence to have some know-it-all asshole suddenly be so essential to her happiness.

She wanted to climb up on his lap, lay her head on his shoulder, and cry.

Would he spank her if she didn't come?

He uncrossed his arms, and he placed his mug on the table, the ceramic scratching along the finished wooden surface, before he rose. She would not stand and wait for him but went to him, meeting him halfway before they collided, but she did not stop. She pushed against him so that he almost lost his balance, his hip hitting the edge of the table. He grabbed her hair and tugged, clumsily undoing the neat bun she'd fastened.

"Fucking hair up," he growled. "You know I don't like that." He pulled her mouth toward him and she whimpered, need and anger battling within her. His lips crushed hers but briefly, a promise and a kiss, before he released her mouth, grasped her elbow, and swung her around, sidestepping so that her belly hit the edge of the table and her hands flailed out in front of her. His palm cracked against her denim-covered ass so hard the sound echoed in the room, then another hard smack left her breathless. He leaned in, his hard, warm body pressed up against her, his breath at her ear, his erection pushed up against her ass.

"Maybe Daddy needs to remind you who you belong to before we go today?" he asked, and something in her clicked. The anger in her chest dissolved, and her eyes watered with tears.

He was going to the fundraiser with her. He still wanted her to belong to him.

She was still his.

She closed her eyes and inhaled so deeply her chest rose, willing herself to calm the nerves that threatened to choke her. No. She would not admit she needed his spanking and his quiet affirmations to ground herself. And what's more, she would *prove* to him that he was wrong, that his accusations against Diana were unfounded.

"No," she grit out, palms squeaking against the glossy tabletop as she pushed herself up, pushed back against him. "I'm good. Really."

He froze behind her but only briefly, before he grasped her waist and spun her around to face him. He tapped a finger under her chin, his gaze meeting hers, stern but conflicted. "You'd better be."

And with that, he released her. As he stalked away, she swallowed her need to cry, squaring her shoulders, her ass still smarting from the sting of his palm. God, she wanted things to be good between them again, but not enough to forgive him so quickly for accusing her mentor of such horrible things when he had no proof. She'd worked her ass off to get where she was, and she couldn't just let it all go while he barked at shadows.

"HEY, TESS," Nora said brightly into the phone.

Tess paused before speaking. "You okay, honey?"

"Yeah, of course I'm okay," Nora said. "Don't be ridiculous. Why?"

Diego gave her a sidelong glance before flicking on the directional and taking a left. Nora huffed out a breath. Was *no one* in her life sane? God!

"You sound... perky," Tessa said. "And usually, perky Nora is dangerous. It means you're either about to break up with someone, ready to read someone the riot act, or go on a deep cleaning binge to deal with whatever's eating you. So... I'm just checking. Perky Nora worries me."

The concern in her sister's voice annoyed Nora, and she scowled out the window. "Since when is saying 'hi' in a friendly manner a matter of concern?" she snapped. Diego squeezed her knee in warning but she shoved his hand off. He slapped her thigh with a sharp smack.

"Ow!"

"Behave yourself," he warned.

"You okay?" Tessa asked. Nora rubbed the sting out of her thigh, instantly subdued and reluctantly turned on, albeit pissed.

"Yeah," she said. "Sorry, Tess."

Diego's warm hand reached for her leg and gently massaged. "Good girl," he whispered. She closed her eyes, fighting against tears that clogged her throat and made her nose tingle.

Why did he have to *call* her that?

But fine. She would focus on the task at hand and stop being a bitch to the people she loved most.

She took a deep breath before speaking into the phone. "I'm just checking to make sure everything's ready for today with the food," she said. "Sorry I snapped. There are so many things that I'm trying to pull together to make sure this all happens, you know? But I'm fine. Diego's taking me in." Though she'd mentioned Diego to Tess before, enough for Tess to know she and Diego were together and things were serious, she hadn't gotten into details. Tessa didn't know she was spending her nights with him, but she didn't really need to know, either. And Tess seemed to have shut off her big-sister need to pry.

"Yeah, babe, I know," Tessa said. "Hey, we're proud of you. You've done an awesome job. Should've heard Tony bragging to the staff last night as they were boxing up the pastries for this morning. Everyone's proud. Allie told me you were a natural. Oh, hey, you heard about Allie, right?"

"Oh yeah, I heard at *Centered* yesterday that Allie went into early labor but they stopped it. She wasn't alone, right?"

"No, Tony and I were around and stayed with the kids, and Slay went to the hospital with her. But she's fine and home now, just on bed rest so she can't make it today."

"Ah. Well I'm glad they stopped labor, though. That's the important thing. Let that little baby Slay cook a little longer."

Tessa laughed. "Yep. Okay so the guys are loading the food into the van now, and Tony and I are delivering it to the field. We threw in some extra salad and dressing, and it'll be well chilled until time to serve. I know that the drinks are already there, and we've got the paper goods and serving utensils packed. All you need to bring is your appetite."

Nora smiled to herself. "Okay, Tess. Thanks so much. Can't wait to see you guys."

She ended the call, then pulled up her email on her phone as Diego spoke. "What's up with Slay?" he asked.

"Allie went into early labor and they had to go to the hospital," she said.

"Yeah, I heard that," he said. Nora frowned. Clearly, the fact they hadn't even discussed it yet underscored just how little they'd seen each other yesterday

"They were able to stop labor and everything's fine now, but I guess Slay stayed with Allie at the hospital all Thursday night, though."

Diego grunted. "She picked a hell of a time to do it." He slowed down as they cruised to a stop at a yellow light. The light turned red, and he turned to her, and his brow furrowed. She smiled, despite her irritation with him.

"Do what? Go into early labor? It happens sometimes," she said. "Not exactly voluntary. Elena explained it to me. Said that sometimes women go into early labor but there are drugs that can sometimes make it stop. And this time, it worked."

Her phone rang and she glanced at the screen.

Diana.

She glanced at Diego sideways as he tapped on the radio. Her phone buzzed a second time, then a third. How would he react?

His lips turned down as he frowned at her. "You gonna answer that, or what?"

"Yes," she said. "I just didn't want to be rude, and—"

"Answer the damn phone."

She scowled at him but tapped the answer button. "Hello? Oh, hi, Diana." She deliberately turned her back on Diego so she wouldn't have to see his stern disapproval. Jerk.

"Hello, Nora. I'm just checking to see if everything is all set? Are you there yet?"

"Yes, I'm on my way now with my..." she paused. What the hell *was* he? The guy she was in love with? Her friend? Her lover. "My boyfriend is driving me. I spoke with Tessa a few minutes ago, and they have the food all set. And it sounds fantastic. Everything is falling into place. We'll make this happen."

"Excellent. Thank you, Nora. I will be there shortly myself, though I have a few things to tend to before I arrive. Are you sure you ordered enough food? And that everything is well taken care of?"

"I-I think so," she said, ignoring the heat of Diego's gaze on her and the way his hand reached for her leg, firmly grasping her thigh. "I did my best, and I'm pretty sure everything will fall into place with us all being there."

"Okay, then. I'll see you soon. And thank you again for all your hard work, Nora. It has been a delight seeing you grow into this role and flourish as you have."

Nora felt a faint flush creep along her cheeks and neck, and she closed her eyes, trying to overcome her emotions at the praise. How could this woman be who Diego said she was? "Thank you. See you soon." She hung up the phone and shoved it in her bag.

"Diana checking in?" Diego asked.

"Yeah. But I don't want to talk about how evil she is or how she's like the underground crime lord of all of the east coast or anything, okay?" The bite of her tone surprised even her, and she half expected him to react, but when she looked at him, he was staring out the window, and not at her. They'd arrived at the rented field where the fund raiser would be held, and he was navigating his car to the furthest corner of the parking area, under a shady patch of weeping willows.

"Really, Diego? Gotta hide over here?"

His lips thinned as he put the car in park and cut the ignition before he turned to face her. Her gaze wandered from his muscled shoulders to the bulge of his biceps, to the way his t-shirt clung to his abs, and his worn jeans straddled his hips. After scoping him out properly, she met his eyes once more, not at all surprised to find them heated. His beard was scruffy and dark, and in the shadow beneath the trees, he looked… dangerous. She shivered, suddenly wishing they were alone and not fighting. Without a word, he opened his door.

Her heartbeat stuttered and her mouth grew dry. She'd been nothing but bitchy to him, and he'd warned her. Would he punish her, right here, in the shade of the trees? He *wouldn't.*

Would he?

He came to her side of the car and opened her door, extending a hand to hers. She allowed him to help her out before he slammed the door shut and pressed the lock button. Still holding her hand, he leaned against the hood and drew her between his legs, shoved his keys in his pocket, then placed his hands on either side of her face.

"Nora," he said. "I want you to listen to me." His brows rose questioningly.

She inhaled, then exhaled. "Yes."

His tone was stern but gentle when he spoke. "I know I said some things the other night that you didn't want to hear. I'm not apologizing for that, and I'm not convinced you're safe yet. But there's no need to have this tension between us. We're on the same team here, babe. You get me?"

Her heart pattered and her belly melted. She nodded. "Yes, Daddy." She could not call him daddy when she was angry or hurt, but it felt nice to say it now.

"I'll sort you out tonight," he said, a promise that made her belly twist and her panties dampen.

"Sort me out?"

"Yeah," he said. "But for now, I want you to know I'm proud of you and that I know you're gonna kill it today."

She smiled. "Thank you."

He pulled her face to his and kissed her forehead. But when he pulled back again, his eyes were darker. "You be careful, honey. I'm going to be in the background, keeping an eye on things. I'm not officially here, yeah? You watch your back. No going off alone with anyone you don't know. No leaving the premises."

She blinked. "Really?"

His grip tightened and his nostrils flared. "*Really.*"

She pulled away from him and shook her head, but he held tight and chucked a finger under her chin. "Behave yourself."

"I will," she said, finally pulling back and walking away. "Enjoy the shadows." He stood behind her, and she felt his gaze following her all the way to the main tent.

Tonight, I'll sort you out.

They'd see about that.

Right now, she had shit to do.

A LARGE TENT stood in the center of a huge, grassy area, a few paces away from a small brick building. Inside was a bathroom, and a table where supplies stood in stacks and boxes, and a small office as well as a pavilion, and a tented area where volunteers had paperwork and information where supporters could gather, and food would be served. There were displays set up with artwork done by the children, all at varying age-levels and complexities, from finger paintings to some incredibly lifelike sketches Camila had done. There was a small set of risers, where the children from *Centered* would perform a few simple songs they'd been studying, set up next to a podium where the Mayor of Boston was going to give a speech about the importance of organizations like *Centered* that brought diversity and acceptance to the community. And mingling throughout the space was a band of volunteers Nora had spent hours training, to the point where they could run the entire afternoon blindfolded.

Nora put her bag just inside the door, shoved her phone in her pocket, and went out to the pavilion where the other volunteers and staffers from *Centered* were assembled.

"Nora, this looks amazing," Elena said. She held her toddler in her arms, and next to her stood her husband Blake, holding the hand of their son.

"Aw, thanks, Elena," Nora said, gathering her hair up in a ponytail so she could get down to business. "You guys have all put in so much effort, and it's looking great here."

"All I wanna know is when Tony gets here with the food," Blake said, patting his stomach. "Someone was too busy to feed her man this morning, and I could eat one of those trays of John's pastries all on my own."

Nora grinned. "You could do that any day, though, Blake," she teased. "I just talked to Tessa, and they're on their way now."

"Nora!" Grace waved her hand from across the way, where she had a table set up with face paints. Nora bid good-bye to Blake and Elena and walked toward the others who were waiting for her. Grace had paper towels, wet wipes, water, and face paints set up next to her, with some hand-drawn pictures of designs the kids could choose from.

"Hey, Camila wants to help with the face paint," Grace said. "Any idea where she is?" Camila had taken to helping Grace with all the art classes at *Centered* over the past week, as she was a natural, and she'd begun to privately speak to Grace and the other women, as well as a therapist. Though she was still shy and hadn't been forthcoming about how she'd arrived in Boston, Nora felt comfortable that she was receiving the best possible care, and that they'd be able to reunite her with her family, or find her a permanent foster care placement, soon.

Nora frowned, guilt pricking at her conscience. She'd been so busy dealing with Diego that she hadn't been able to see Camila as much as she would have liked over the past few days. "I don't know," she said. "I'm sorry I've been out of the loop."

Grace wiped her hand on a wet wipe and picked up her pencil, beginning another sketch. "No worries, honey. Gosh, I bet pulling together all these details the past few days has been totally consuming, huh?"

Nora nodded. *Pulling together all these details and dealing with a bossy daddy, yeah.* "I'll ask around and see if anyone knows where she is, okay?"

A familiar white van pulled up and Nora waved goodbye to Grace. The delivery from *Cara* had arrived. When the passenger door opened and Tessa stepped out, Nora felt her throat tighten at the sight. Tessa had been with her through *everything*. All of it. From leaving her mother's and moving in with her and Tony, to graduating from college, to finding full-time work and finding her place in the workforce. Tessa had wiped her tears, paid her bills, and listened to her in the wee hours of the morning when the world slept and her mind churned. How she wanted to pour her heart out to her big sister.

Tessa's auburn hair was high up in a clip, and she was running a lip gloss brush over her lips. "Hey, babe!" she said, waving, and when Nora drew closer, Tessa's perceptive gaze narrowed. "Are you okay?" she asked. The lump in Nora's throat grew and her nose stung. She swallowed and cleared her throat.

"Hey," she said.

Tessa reached for her, snaking an arm around her waist and pulling her close. She gave her a tight, motherly hug and one lone tear splashed on Nora's cheek. She swiped it impatiently away.

"I'm fine," she lied, but Tessa knew her too well.

"The hell you are," she whispered in her ear. "And something tells me this has nothing to do with work or the people here, and everything to do with that sweet, maddening bossman of yours, huh?"

Nora nodded, and she thought for a minute maybe it *would* be okay to tell Tessa everything. But how could she? The information she'd gotten from Diego about Diana was confidential. Though it would feel so good to divulge it all, and get it all off her chest, she could not put anyone at risk. For a moment, she wondered how hard it had to have been for Diego to hold it all on his own for so long. Yeah, he had guys like Slay who knew, but were there things he held onto that he didn't tell anyone? Things that he had to keep to himself, for the safety of others?

If he could be brave, so could she. She swallowed her tears and took a deep, cleansing breath. "Hey," she said to Tessa. "Some days are just hard, you know? But it's all good. Really."

Tessa released Nora from her embrace but held her at arm's length, peering into her eyes like only a big sister could. "They are," she said. "And you don't need to tell me everything. Two people, both learning who the other is… you get the good with the bad. But if it's meant to be, and you learn to give without losing who you are, it makes you stronger." She paused, and drew in a deep breath. "But I know who you are, Nora Damon. I've seen you overcome shit that would've made other girls crumple. But not you, honey. Whatever it is that's eating you up? You'll handle it. Because that's what Nora Damon does." Tessa leaned over to swipe one more tear from Nora's cheek, and Nora wondered if Diego had seen their interaction. What was *he* thinking? What was going on in his mind?

And in that moment, she forgave him. Tessa was right. This was the give and take, and if she and Diego were meant to be, then hell, they'd make their way through this shit and they'd be stronger. She wished she could find him then, to bury her head on his chest and let him hold her, so she could call him daddy and find strength in him… in *them*.

As Nora turned around, she saw the young girl walking side-by-side with Grace. Camila smiled and waved at Nora.

"Oh, you found her!" Nora shouted, as Tony opened the back of the white van and lifted out two large white pastry boxes.

"Where are these going, Nora the Explorer?" Tony asked. Nora smirked at the pet name Tony had given her when he'd adopted her as his little sister, and pointed to where the empty tables lay under the big tents.

"Over there, on those tables. Thanks, Tony." She turned back to Grace and Camila, and as she did, a gleaming black car pulled in right up at the entrance to the fairgrounds. The guest speakers, including the mayor, weren't due for another hour. And as she waited for the driver to go around to open the door, she saw a shadow lurking beneath the weeping willows at the far side of the lot where Diego had parked. Diego leaned against the door, his arms across his chest. She couldn't quite tell with the distance and his face cast in shadow, but it looked like he winked at her. A small thrill of pleasure rippled through her, just as the door to the car opened, and out stepped Diana.

"Oh, hi! Good to see you," Nora greeted Diana, fervently hoping that everything was all set for the fundraiser now, so that it looked perfect. "You're early!"

Diana smiled warmly. "Hello, Nora. So pleased to see you," she said, extending her hand, and as Nora shook it in reply, she wondered if Diego could see them. Was he plotting a way to sweep in and save her in case his instincts were right?

"The caterers just arrived and are setting up. I can guarantee the food will be delicious. My brother-in-law Tony is one of the best chefs in Boston," she bragged, just as Grace and Camila strolled towards them.

"Oh I can attest to that," Grace said with a laugh. "I've sampled just about everything on the menu at *Cara*." She turned to Nora. "Hey, Camila and I are going to get started on the face painting, since kids are starting to arrive with their parents. Sound good?"

"Awesome," Nora said. "Diana, I'll show you to where the office is so you can put your stuff away." As Grace and Camila left, Nora turned toward Diana and was surprised to see her gaze was fixed on Camila, a smile frozen on her face.

"What did you say the girl's name was?" she asked, her voice unusually high. Nora's heartbeat raced.

No. No, Diego was wrong. He had to be... His paranoia was affecting her ability to function as a normal human being, damnit.

Nora cleared her throat. "Camila," she said.

Diana smiled warmly. "A lovely name. And she's one of your clients? She's new, isn't she?" Diana slung her bag over her shoulder as her driver went to park the car.

"She is," Nora said. "She's only just come to us recently, and we don't fully know what her story is, but we will do everything we can to help her."

Diana blinked, and her smile brightened. "You don't know her story?" she asked.

Nora's stomach clenched, and the back of her neck prickled. *Diego is crying wolf,* she told herself. *It doesn't even make logical sense. And now he's fucking with your mind and your own imagination is running wild.*

"Yes," she said. She had to change the subject. "Okay so the office is over here. Follow me." As she walked toward the office, Diana joined her. "You could have some privacy here if need be," Nora said. They walked past the boxes and supplies, and Diana nodded.

"Excellent," she said. "This is perfect, thank you. If you'll excuse me, I have some phone calls to make." She smiled, but her eyes looked... colder. Nora mentally shook herself. *Diego had made her crazy.*

"Nora!" a voice came from right outside the door, so she left Diana and went outside, and saw Tessa gesturing to her from across the lot, panic in her eyes. Tony held a blood-stained paper towel to his hand.

"Oh my God! Tony, what did you do? Are you okay?" Nora asked.

"Cut my damn hand," he muttered sheepishly.

Tessa hovered over him. "I told you not to cut that with the stupid knife," she muttered, and he shook his head as she turned to Nora. "He's always cutting those boxes open with the knife, and I keep telling him, one of these days—"

"Babe, I'm fine," Tony said. "Just looks like I need a band-aid. Knock it off."

Tessa blew out a breath and glared at him, and he gave her a sheepish grin, but then raised a brow. She shook her head. "Maddening Angelico brother," Tessa muttered. "Nora, do you guys have first aid supplies here?"

"Yes, back in the office," she said. "Just a minute." She hurried to the office, expecting to see the door shut tight, but instead the door to the office stood ajar. The first aid kit sat on a shelf in the office just a few paces away, but as Nora went to retrieve it, she froze. Someone was in there. At the sound of Diana's voice, Nora flattened herself against the wall outside. Her voice was barely audible, and after her pauses no one replied, so Nora could easily surmise she was talking on the phone. The tone sent a shiver of fear down her spine.

"She's here," Diana spat out. "I saw her with my own eyes. Who? You idiot. The girl who escaped. The girl who could ruin everything. Her name is *Camila*."

Nora closed her eyes, frozen in place, her heart pounding so loudly she feared Diana would hear it. Oh, God.

Diego had been right. Fucking hell, Diego had been *right*.

Diana continued. "I don't know how much she knows, but Padre's whole operation is compromised. Bah! Padre. I can't believe I ever trusted him. I won't have this blowing back on me, Miguel." A pregnant pause, and then, "I'll take care of the girl. You know what you have to do. Yes. Destroy the warehouse and the entire Boston operation. Wipe it out. Wipe them *all* out, even Padre. Make it look like an accident."

Padre.

Nora didn't stay to hear more. Her heart in her throat, her

palms sweaty, her vision blurred, she raced through the doorway to Tessa and Tony. "Come with me," she said. Tessa was too busy helping Tony with his hand and thankfully they seemed oblivious to Nora's anxiety.

She smiled brightly to hide her fear as she walked to the face painting table to fetch Camila, and for a moment she panicked. *Where was Camila?* She couldn't see her anywhere. Grace sat with a line of children waiting to have their faces painted, but the chair where Camila had sat was vacant. Nora feigned nonchalance, brushing her hair off her shoulder as she walked over, leaned in, and whispered to Grace, "Hey, have you seen Camila?"

"Sure," Grace said. "She went to the concessions to get us drinks."

"Ah, okay," Grace said. "Well, I need to run a quick errand with her, so I'm going to take her with me."

"Okay," Grace said. Grace smiled at the little boy sitting on a folding chair in front of her. "Spiderman, you said?"

Nora turned away. What if she was too late? What if Diana's assistant had already taken Camila? Tessa waved frantically from where she stood tending to Tony, and Nora held up her hand, gesturing for her to wait.

She had to find Camila. Turning to the concessions, she scanned frantically but didn't see her. Guests had begun to arrive in droves, and the parking lot teemed with minivans and cars. Nora walked through the crowd, ignoring those who called out to her or tried to stop her, bent on finding the girl and getting her the hell out of there.

She picked up her cell and dialed.

"Everything okay, babe?" Diego's voice made sudden tears spring to her eyes. He'd been right. The whole time, he'd been right and her own pride had made her blind. What if it was too late?

"No, it's not," she choked.

What if his phone was tapped? What if right at this very minute, Diana was at her back, activating her men?

"What? Nora, where are you?" His voice hardened and she could picture the look on his face, eyes alert, shoulders back, ready to crack skulls.

"Over by the concessions," she said, forcing a smile at a couple who waved to her, and then she saw Camila. Hope welled in her chest. Camila leaned over a cooler, brushing ice off two cans of soda. "You still here?"

"Yes. Are you okay?"

"Yes. But I need your help. You were right about Diana."

A brief pause. "Baby, be careful. I'm in the parking lot. Hurry."

She hung up the phone and walked quickly to Camila, keeping her head down, her imagination running wild. The man standing next to the little boy with the popcorn—were his eyes on her? Was he Diana's henchman, and was he telling Diana right now what Nora was doing? Did someone *right now* have their sights on Diego? Would they find him? She needed him out of here. If she took Camila to him now and any of Diana's men saw them…

She grabbed Camila's hand. "Hi, honey. I need to run an errand. Come with me?"

Camila pointed towards Grace, but Nora shook her head. "No," she said. "You *have* to come with me. Okay?" her smile felt fake, plastered on her face, but she wasn't taking no for an answer.

"Nora!" someone called from behind, but Nora tightened her grip on Camila, and pulled her toward the parking lot where Tess stood with Tony.

"Come on, guys," Nora said. "Diego's coming, and he'll take us to the hospital."

Her phone buzzed insistently in her bag, but she ignored it.

She saw Diego's car turning round the lot and coming to where they stood.

Tessa frowned. "Nora, what's going on?" she asked, just as Diego pulled up. Nora imagined Diana behind her now, her henchmen at their heels. They'd have their sights on Camila, and they wouldn't let her go. Everything seemed to be in slow motion as Nora moved, as Camila shook her head, insisting she needed to stay, and Tessa stared at them both in confusion.

"Camila," she said quietly, insistently. "Padre is here. He will keep you safe." She tugged on the side door and practically shoved Camila in. "You guys too," she ordered Tess and Tony. She caught the barest glimmer of Diego's concerned look as they all got in the car, then she trotted to the passenger seat, jumped in and slammed the door.

"Nora!" The voice was muffled by the sound of the engine, and Nora didn't look back, but she felt the hairs on her arms raise. Diana's voice rang through the crowd again. "*Nora!*"

She willed herself to stay calm, focusing on Diego.

"Nora, what's going on?" Tessa asked again as Diego reached for Nora's knee and squeezed. She calmed and took a deep breath.

"I'll tell you in a minute. For now, *go. Fast*," she said.

"*Madre de Dios*," Diego muttered, but without another word he accelerated, and seconds later, they pulled into a busy intersection.

"Tony cut his hand opening a box and needs stitches," she said to Diego, and, urgently, "You were right. About Diana, about everything. I overheard her on a phone call and I think your life and Camila's are both in jeopardy. They could be coming for us any minute." She inhaled deeply as he revved the engine. "*Go!*"

Chapter 9

"I don't give a shit what you think you know," Diego spat into his phone, ignoring the warning looks cast at him by the older couple who sat at the far end of the otherwise-deserted hospital waiting room just down the hall from the ER where Nora and her family sat. "I'm telling you what's happening!"

"Listen, Santiago, I'm doing my best." The voice on the other end of the line sounded frustrated and more than a little overwhelmed. Feebs were notoriously in love with their bureaucracy and rule-following, and both Slay and Diego had run across a few handlers who'd made their lives difficult over the years, but Michael Darby, Slay's brand new contact at the FBI, seemed to have come from a different planet—one where human lives meant jack shit.

Diego spared a moment to imagine just how much control and patience Slay must have expended in dealing with this idiot for the past week, as Darby continued, "We have two other ongoing operations that have both come to a head this weekend. I don't have the resources to go on your little fact-finding mission. I told Slater—"

"And I told *you*, Slay's not *fucking* here right now," Diego reminded the man. He didn't care that his voice had gotten louder and was glad when the older couple gathered their belongings and left in a huff. He removed the door stop and closed the waiting room door behind them so he could have privacy. His language was the least of his concerns tonight, but it was probably for the best that he not have any witnesses for the things he was about to say.

"He left you all of the information you needed to pick up the slack on the operations he was working with you, and you've fucking failed at every turn. Tomás Guttierez is dead thanks to your team's ineptitude." Diego could hear his own voice nearly crack with the strain and forced himself to take a deep breath. Blaming Darby wouldn't bring Tomás back, but the tightly-coiled anger in Diego's belly needed an outlet, and this asshole was as good as any.

"That's not fair," Darby argued. "As soon as Slater alerted us that he wouldn't be on-scene to handle the takedown Thursday night, we notified the police that they should keep Mr. Guttierez separated from the general population. The fact that the dispatcher didn't alert the correct people is not a situation we could have foreseen."

"Yeah, right," Diego said bitterly. "Except you didn't *have* to foresee it, because Slay alerted you when he knew his wife was going into labor and he wouldn't be around for the mission. He gave you the name of his contact at the Wilmington PD and specifically told you that you'd need to call the guy personally. But did you? Nope. You figured, why bother listening to the guy who's been running this op for years? You might as well have called the freakin' *janitor* over there for all the good you did."

"Fuck you, Santiago. I think you've been under too long, buddy. You forget how shit is supposed to work. You report your findings to your contact person, namely *me*. I provide the information to my superior, Berkley Carrerra, the AIC of the Boston Office. That stands for…"

"I know what a fucking AIC is, Darby! And I don't give a shit if your buddy Berkley is the Agent in Charge or the second coming of Christ!" Diego whispered furiously. "I'm telling you, shit is going down tonight. Lives are in *danger.*"

"Because your girlfriend overheard something." Darby had the balls to sound dubious about the accuracy of what Nora overheard, and Diego wished he had a clue what this smug motherfucker looked like so he could better visualize his fist hitting Darby's face.

"Because an intelligent, reliable witness overheard it," he said.

Darby sighed. "Santiago," he began in an even more placating tone. "Even if I didn't have any questions about the accuracy of what you overheard… And maybe everything Miss Damon heard *was* accurate," he was quick to say, as though he could hear Diego grinding his teeth over the phone connection. "We don't know what El Jefe was really talking about when he… *shit…* I mean *she* said that she was dismantling the whole Boston operation. Maybe he… er, *she*… meant that she was just going to abandon the warehouse, or…"

"*Take everyone out, even Padre?*" Diego reminded him of the words Nora had overheard. He held his jaw so tightly it was a wonder his teeth didn't crack.

Darby, the fucking useless piece of shit, just sighed again, like this was all too much for him. "I'm telling you, I don't have the resources. Now, I can put you in touch with a guy on the local PD, you can tell him your story and…"

"You know what, Darby?" Diego said. "Don't fucking bother." He was done. So fucking done. Completely burned out with the bureaucracy, the hierarchy, and the stupid minutiae that threatened to derail this investigation just when it seemed like they might finally seal the deal. But he couldn't resist adding, before hanging up the phone, "But if anyone dies at that warehouse tonight, that's on *you*."

"I gather that you've had the pleasure of speaking with Michael Darby?" a voice from the doorway asked, and Diego glanced over to see Slay, looking more tired than Diego had ever seen him, holding open the waiting room door, with Matteo by his side.

"Slay!" Diego said in annoyed surprise. "Man, I told you…"

"Yeah," Slay replied, holding out a hand as if to stem the tide of Diego's argument. "You told me to stay home with Allie. I appreciate it, but I'm good. The other night was a different story —I had no clue what was going on, and I needed to be there for my girl. And even right afterward, Allie was a bundle of nerves. She needed me, and you know that's my priority."

Diego nodded. He'd have made the same call if Nora needed him. Hell, he *had* made that call.

"But now, the doctor says everything is stable. As long as she's in bed, she's fine. And as of this morning, Allie's mom has moved into the spare bedroom for the duration and she's cleaning fucking *everything*," he said with a wince that made Diego stifle a grin. "I love her, and Alice does too. And we need the help with the boys. But after a couple hours, Allie told me to get out of the house before I lost my mind. She's a smart cookie."

Matteo laughed, and Slay lifted an eyebrow to glare at him, which only made Matt chuckle harder.

"Not busting on you, man," Matteo argued. "I'm laughing cause I get it. Hillie's mom *and* dad came to stay with us after our oldest was born. They *were* fucking divorced, but now that they're remarried, those two don't move two feet without holding hands," he grumbled, rolling his eyes. "Anyway, I knew Hillie needed the help and was glad to have them there, so I bit my tongue and let her mom make us all kinds of herbal teas and shit to *balance our energies*." He shuddered.

Diego snorted, shaking his head. He'd been ready to explode

a minute ago, but just imagining Matteo sucking down herbal tea under his hippie mother-in-law's watchful eye helped to calm the worst of the anger. He sucked in a deep breath.

"Better?" Slay asked knowingly.

"I don't know how you put up with assholes like that all these years." Diego shook his head. "Just one phone call and I was nearly through the roof."

"Well, Darby is a particularly bad example. That guy couldn't be more inept if he were playing for the other side. But now you see why I prefer being a security contractor who works *with* the FBI instead of an agent."

"Yeah," Diego said morosely. "But now we have no backup and no authority to move on this in an official capacity, and given what Nora overheard today, shit is going down tonight. A dozen more lives are on the line. Lives of guys who deserve justice but don't deserve to die the way Tomás did. And if we let Diana leave town without gaining evidence to tie her to her crimes, we lose our chance of catching El Jefe for good."

"About that…" Matteo grinned. "You remember I have the best sister-in-law ever, right? Well… actually, I have a couple of them, but only one of them is a crazy-awesome forensic accountant."

Diego's eyes widened. "Heidi found something?"

Matt nodded. "She and Paul have been working like crazy the past few days, and she figured out your crazy idea about Diana wasn't crazy at all, even before the bitch went all psycho-kidnapper at the fundraiser. Also turns out, Paul's been hiding some sick-ass hacking skills. We found some pictures of Diana Consuelos, aka Diana Jimenez, aka Carmen Escobar, from some arrest records in San Diego and Reno."

Diego's eyes widened, and Slay nodded. "Turns out this isn't El Jefe's first rodeo. She was a madam in a prostitution ring on the west coast for years, but when she was busted, she turned state's evidence against a couple of guys higher up the food chain. She did time in a minimum-security place in the Midwest, far away from her previous associates, who were all convicted and are serving serious time in maximum-security facilities."

"Meaning Diana is persona non grata out west," Matteo confirmed. "But they loved her in prison. She was a model of good behavior and her five-year stint was shortened to eighteen months."

"Fucking bullshit," Slay said, outraged. "But apparently they felt she'd reformed."

"Joke's on them, because she never *stopped* scamming," Matt told them. "The bulk of the money from the prostitution ring was never recovered, and Uncle Sam assumed that it had been funneled offshore by one of the guys before his arrest. But Paul was able to trace that money through some dummy corporations and tax shelters to Consuelos Imports, Ltd. Diana had started up her next criminal organization while she was still in fucking prison." He shook his head.

"You can tie the prostitution money to Diana's company?" Diego breathed. "That simple?" El Jefe had been three steps ahead of them all this time. Was it possible she could have done something so stupid?

Slay shrugged, and his lips quirked. "That simple. Like Al Capone with the tax evasion. Or like Chalo Salazar getting sent down for insurance fraud instead of drug running or the billions of other illegal things he did. Diana probably had no idea how big she'd one day become when this first started. And then, once she had a large, successful company behind her, and a reputation as a successful businesswoman and philanthropist to back her up, she must have figured she was untouchable."

"And she would have gotten away with it, too, if it weren't for you meddling kids," Matteo said in his best Scooby-Doo villain voice, making Slay roll his eyes and shake his head. "Seriously, though, not one person in a thousand would have thought to look where you did, Diego."

Diego shook off the praise and focused on the facts. "Have you passed all of this on to Darby?" he demanded. "When do we get a warrant? When can we move?"

Slay and Matteo exchanged a glance. "About that..."

"What?" Diego asked uneasily, looking between the two.

"Well, we *could* call Darby," Matteo said. "We could ask *him* to obtain authorization from his AIC to apply for a warrant, and then wait for a warrant to come through, and then wait for them to assemble a team, even though apparently we're low on their priority list and shit's going down in a matter of hours."

"Or? Please tell me there's an *or* here..." Diego stared at Slay.

Slay smiled. "*Or*... we could call in a favor with a friend. Turns out Lucas has a friend who works with the Director of the FBI, way above Darby and his AIC. And if that weren't enough, Allie's dad is poker buddies with a guy who happens to be a bailiff at the Federal court, and knows a couple of judges..."

"So we can get a warrant? And authorization?" Diego asked.

Matt nodded. "Still no FBI backup, which means limited resources that make this a lot more dangerous. And when Darby and *Berkley* find out about this, I wouldn't be surprised if they find a way to blacklist us with the FBI once and for all, but..." He hesitated. "Fuck it. Some things are just worth the risk. I know *you* know that." He clapped Diego on the shoulder. "I trust you, Santiago. I want you to be point man for this op."

Fuck, yeah, Diego knew all about taking risks. In fact, he'd been ready to fight Darby tooth and nail just to be allowed to be *on* the takedown team. Now it appeared he'd be leading it.

"So, you and me?" Diego said. "We can go in stealthily, and..."

Slay folded his hands over his chest and shook his head. "Shut up. You think I'd let you two do this alone? When I think of Camila and what could've happened to her if you hadn't gotten her free... I want in on this. And I've called all the guys on my team for a meeting at headquarters in two hours. I know for a fact that they're gonna want to be a part of this too."

"*All* the guys?" Diego asked, honestly confused. "Why? Most of them haven't met Camila, and they have no clue about El Jefe's operation. If Darby and Berkley get their panties in a bunch, every guy who takes part tonight could be blacklisted from future FBI-connected ops. Why would they want to risk themselves for this?"

"You don't get it, do you?" Slay said, shaking his head and watching Diego with those brown eyes that saw fucking everything. "I've told you a hundred times and you won't believe me."

Diego glanced at Matteo, who watched the exchange with a smirk on his lips. Matteo's phone rang and he stepped away to answer it, but Slay's eyes didn't waver from Diego.

"Believe what?" Diego asked.

"Believe that *I see who you are*. That Nora sees you. That all the guys who work with us, and all the people you've met at The Club, they see you too. Blake and Elena and Dom and Heidi, all of them, all of *us*, see you. You're not a criminal. You're not a man with blood on his hands. You're a good man who's had to do some incredibly awful stuff." He shook his head. "I mean, shit that's gonna haunt your nightmares for the rest of your fucking life. But you did it so that the rest of us could sleep soundly in our beds, so that our kids can breathe a little more freely, so that our wives and partners can feel just a little bit safer and worry about us a little bit less when we go out to work. And by your instincts alone in this op, you found the one clue that could take down a crime boss and saved hundreds, maybe *thousands,* of lives. If you think you need a penance for something? If you think you need to balance the scales? Brother, they're already balanced."

Diego closed his eyes and sucked in a breath. It was impossible for him to articulate just what Slay's words, Slay's confidence, meant to him, but now wasn't the time or the place for him to get sucked into that shit. "Jesus, enough."

Slay, the fucker, laughed loud and long at Diego's discomfort.

Diego rolled his eyes. "I've gotta find Nora and Camila. I left them hanging with Tony, Tess, Dom, and Heidi in the family waiting room outside the ER."

"I checked on them before I came in," Slay said. "I asked Tony if he needed me to hold his hand while they stitched him up, and Matt reminded him that if he was going to pass out, he should lean *away* from Tess."

Diego laughed despite himself. Pair of smartasses. He went to move past Slay, but the other man stopped him with a hand on Diego's shoulder. Slay's mouth twisted up on one side. "I should've believed you from the start about this. Shoulda trusted your instincts."

Something inside Diego's chest loosened at that acknowledgement, but he shook his head and stepped forward to clap Slay on the shoulder. "You believed me where it counted, and you put Paul and Heidi on this. And if you'd kept Diana away from *Centered*, it might have tipped her hand."

"Yep. But I could've made sure all of that happened while still letting you know that I trusted your gut. When I'm wrong, I say I'm wrong."

"And when you're an asshole, do you say you're an asshole?" Matt asked, stepping back into the room. Slay raised an eyebrow at him, and Matt chuckled before sobering. "That was Lucas. It's a go."

Slay nodded. "I'm calling Allie's dad."

Diego's gut clenched. *Finally.* Things had started to go right with this operation. Thoughts of Camila and all the girls who had come before her flashed through his mind, along with images of his brother Armando, his mother, Nora, Tomás. *I'm going to end this tonight*, he vowed. *For all of you. For all of us.*

WHEN HE STEPPED out of the waiting room, he saw Nora was already walking down the hall towards him. Her face brightened when she caught sight of him, but Diego frowned. "Babe, you shouldn't be wandering around alone. Not now," he warned. "It's not safe."

"I was looking for you. I wondered where you'd gone off to, and whether you'd learned anything more about…"

"Nora, I told you to stay with Tony and Dom," he interrupted, folding his arms over his chest. "Remember?"

"Diego, it's a hospital hallway," she said, and he could hear the eye-roll in her voice. "I think I'm pretty safe, between the security cameras and the people walking around!"

He sucked in a breath. The relief he felt at the knowledge that this chapter of his career would be ending tonight once and for all, was tempered by the very real fear he felt about Nora's safety—especially given that El Jefe planned to tie up all her loose ends in Boston and that Nora had shown *again* that she would not heed his warnings.

He would teach the woman to listen to him, one way or another.

"Yeah, you're probably right," he lied easily. He lowered his arms and wrapped one around her waist, then turned her back in the direction she'd come. "I mean, if something happened to you, someone would see, wouldn't they?"

She nodded, relieved. "Exactly, I mean—"

Her last word ended with a squeak as Diego pulled her into an unlocked maintenance closet he'd noticed earlier. Before she could take a breath or finish her sentence, he had spun her around so that her cheek was flush against the metal surface of the closed door, both of her hands trapped in one of his. He pressed the length of his chest against her back.

"You were saying?" he whispered in her ear.

"Daddy! What are you doing!" she demanded, struggling against the awkward position. "Let me go."

"Let you go? Why? Nothing bad can happen to you when you're walking down a hospital hallway, right?" One of his hands snaked into the waistband of her jeans, flicking the button open, while the other continued to pin her wrists. "And if you don't know what I'm doing, *mamita*, you haven't been paying attention."

She abruptly stopped struggling, stopped moving altogether, and for one short moment, he listened to her breathing fast and excited. "You with me, Nora?" he asked, and she nodded.

He pressed her wrists to the door once, a reminder for her to leave them there, then released them. His hands now roamed her body—over the smooth, firm line of her abdomen, over her lush hips, and came to rest on her round ass.

"The past few days, things have been strained between us. I'm your Daddy," he said, his voice gravelly and low as he kneaded her soft flesh. "And you have no idea how badly I wanted to remind you—to remind *both of us*—of that fact. We work better when we remember our roles."

He gathered her hair in one hand and used it to tilt her head to the side, allowing him unfettered access to the sensitive skin below her ear, and then used that access to torture her mercilessly with his tongue and teeth. "Our relationship, the *trust* between us, they're new and fragile, and I know I can't force them. So even though I've seen you pulling away from me, struggling with the information I gave you, pushing all my buttons, I deliberately haven't pushed you, haven't punished you, haven't spanked you. You needed time to remember why you trusted me in the first place, and I wanted you to have that. But when it mattered, baby? When push came to shove and you needed to make a decision that would protect you and Camila, you didn't hesitate. You trusted your daddy instinctively, didn't you?"

"Yes, Daddy," she whispered.

He nodded against her neck. "You've made your decision.

And now there's no going back. From now on, when you disobey, there will be consequences."

She caught her lip between her teeth and watched him over her shoulder through heavy-lidded eyes. *Christ*. The woman was aroused. He knew if he dipped his hands inside her panties right now, he'd find her wet and wanting.

He sucked in a deep breath and adjusted his rapidly swelling cock in his pants. First things first.

"Were you supposed to be walking in the hall?" he demanded, pulling her hips away from the door and positioning her so that she was tilted at an angle, supported by her hands. "When El Jefe is still out there, still gunning for us?"

"No," she whispered, resigned.

He pulled her jeans and panties down her legs in one quick motion. "That's right," he agreed.

And then he brought his palm down on her ass with a *crack* so loud that it echoed in the small space. Nora let out a muffled whimper. "You stay quiet, baby," he whispered in her ear. "Unless you *want* someone to come in here?"

She swallowed and shook her head, but when she glanced over her shoulder at him, her eyes were dilated and her cheeks flushed with unmistakable arousal. *Fuck*. So many things about this woman enflamed him, so many things he couldn't wait to explore... once he knew for sure that she was safe.

Crack, crack, crack. Nora jumped with each blow, but stayed silent.

"What is my number one priority?" he demanded.

"M-me?" she guessed.

He brought his hand down once more. "There is no question about that, Nora. You are my first and *only* priority. Everything I do, every fucking thing from here on out, will be focused on keeping you safe and happy. But I can't do that unless you take my warnings seriously and obey me. Do you understand?"

"Yes, Daddy," she said softly.

He hated punishing her when she responded so sweetly, when her "*Yes, Daddy*" made his head swim with the need to pull her back against him and claim her fully. But he knew that if she didn't learn to heed his warnings, he could lose her, and that was completely unacceptable.

Slap. He brought his hand down against her rapidly warming flesh over and over again, loving the way her skin grew rosy pink in the dim overhead light, thrilling at the knowledge that her body would wear his mark. Only ever *his* mark.

She had buried her face in her arm after the first few swats, likely to keep herself quiet, but he could tell from the hitch in her breathing that she was crying or on the verge. He ran his palms over her tender skin and put his nose against her neck. "You're so brave, my good girl. Such a sweet, brave girl taking your punishment from me."

She pulled her head up and turned her head until her eyes—wide, wet, and utterly wrecked—met his. "I'm sorry, Daddy," she said, and he nodded.

"I know, baby. I know. And now Daddy's going to make you feel better."

He kissed her jaw lightly before dropping to his knees behind her and guiding her feet out of her shoes and jeans until her lower half was completely naked. He pressed his open mouth to the scalding hot skin of her ass as she braced herself against the door, sliding his tongue against the tender flesh. "Daddy made you ache and now Daddy will take the ache away."

He pushed his hand against her lower back so that her pussy arched towards his mouth and she widened her legs eagerly. He stroked a finger through her folds. She trembled against him, and he felt an answering pulse in his cock. Then he dipped his head the final inch and licked her, suckling her tiny bud between his lips. She cried out softly, and he lost himself in the sweet, warm wonder of her.

It wasn't long before she was bucking against him, riding his mouth. The sounds coming out of her throat were deep, uninhibited, and *loud*, and he could feel his erection straining against his jeans, growing more superbly painful and insistent with each of her cries. Some dim part of his brain reminded him that he should warn her to be quiet, but he'd become a creature of instinct. *Let them hear. Let them know exactly who I am to her.*

A moment later, he stood up and, for the first time, reached for the opening of his own jeans, pulling them down to his thighs. Then he slid himself into the slick warmth of her.

The air was filled with twin moans—hers and his, and his heart thumped hard at the ineffable sense of rightness that came over him. The sense of *home*.

Home was not his mother's house, with its reminders of happier times. It wasn't the crew where his brother Armando had died, or the job he'd taken on as penance. It wasn't even the group of friends who Slay said *saw him*. Home was Nora. Home was being a daddy to his good girl.

He braced one of his hands on the door next to hers, while the other arched around her body to find her clit. "Do you feel that, baby?" he demanded, his voice absolutely ruined with lust and emotion. "That's something that only you and I will ever have together."

"It's perfect," she breathed, her voice high and filled with wonder.

"It's *us*," he said simply. And then he began to move inside her, harder and faster, until time spun out and he forgot everything but the beauty of Nora and the utter completeness they found together.

OF COURSE, the sense of peace he'd found with Nora in that little closet hadn't lasted forever. By the time they'd emerged and gone to find Tony and Tess, Nora blushing and stammering as she tried to explain their sudden disappearance, Diego's mind had already turned towards the final chapter in the years-long saga of his life undercover, a chapter that would end tonight.

He'd brought Nora to Dom and Heidi's house, where she'd be able to hang with her friends Tony, Tess, Hillie, Donnie, Grace, Elena, Blake, Paul, John, and several of the wives and partners of Slay's crew members who were working the op with them.

"Only *this* family would throw a fucking party while your men work an op," Blake had grumbled to Slay when they'd descended on the eldest Angelico's large suburban home. In truth, Diego knew that Blake was glad they were together, and glad to do his part by keeping the families of the men taking part in the operation safe.

And thanks to their interlude in the supply closet, Diego knew that Nora would certainly do her part to stay safe, as well.

A smirk rose to his lips, but he bit it back. *Mind on the job, so you can get back to your woman.* Diego reminded himself as Matteo slowly drove their unmarked black van down the street towards the warehouse.

With a sigh, Diego pushed the button on the tiny device inside his ear. "Slay, gimme an update."

"Thirteen units in place around the building," Slay relayed, his voice loud and clear in Diego's ear. Diego knew that in reality, Slay's voice was nothing more than a whisper of sound, amplified by the advanced communications devices they wore. "Three men on the rooftops—two snipers and one working comms. Four of us in place at the front entrance, five at the rear entrance near the harbor, and Jones is hovering on a fire escape, prepared to breach. We're ready to go once you're in position."

Diego nodded to himself, then realizing Slay couldn't see him, he said aloud, "Good. And the men from Salazar's crew?"

"All gathered inside," Slay told him. "Eleven men total." Eleven, not twelve. Diego thought of Tomás, the misguided, arrogant fucker, and his heart squeezed. "We have ears inside the warehouse, and we overheard a couple of them grumbling that Banyon had gotten a call from El Jefe this afternoon, and had sent out word to all of the other guys. They're all speculating about why the number three guy had gotten the call, rather than you or Tomás." Slay paused. "They're speculating that you're dead by El Jefe's hand over the missing girl, and they're wondering if tonight will be the night that El Jefe reveals himself."

Diego grunted. He couldn't blame the men for their suspicions. He'd received his own summons from El Jefe this afternoon, informing that they would need to meet at the warehouse to discuss "contingency plans" for "handling Camila," and he'd known immediately that any *contingency plan* would not involve Diego's continued existence on the planet. Still, he also knew that a woman as smart as Diana Consuelos would not set this final phase of her plan into motion until she knew that all of her intended targets—including him—were inside the building, so here he was... live bait.

"Speaking of," Slay continued. "The guys did a check of the building when we arrived. Everything's set up exactly as we expected. And no sign of any explosives. However that lunatic plans to destroy the warehouse, it's not going to involve any dramatic fireworks."

Diego made a noise of agreement. He hadn't really anticipated that Diana Consuelos would do something as dramatic and attention-grabbing as an explosion—far too many questions to answer after that. But he'd needed to cover all the bases, for everyone's sake.

He'd thought long and hard about how Diana's dismantling *was* going to go down before he and Slay had finally worked out a plan. They couldn't imagine Diana would reveal herself to the men in the warehouse—not only was it not her style, Diego was fairly sure that most of the crew would mutiny when they learned that the *man* they'd respected and feared was actually a fairly attractive middle-aged *woman*. But Diego, Slay, and the team were also banking on the idea that after so many screw ups and near-misses, El Jefe would not totally trust the person on the other end of the phone call Nora had overheard to plan and carry out something as crucial as the destruction of Padre's entire Boston operation. Not without Diana's active involvement. If the warehouse were about to be destroyed and the men inside killed, Diana would be nearby to give the final order herself… and to watch their world burn.

Matteo pulled the van to the curb four blocks back from the warehouse and immediately killed the lights. He turned and looked at Diego expectantly.

The street was dark with only a few dimly flickering streetlights functioning, and Diego grabbed his phone to check the time. Seven-twenty. "Ten minutes to show time," he whispered. "I'm exiting the vehicle."

"Roger that," Slay confirmed.

Diego continued, "Lucas and Matt, get into position for the extraction. I'm going silent for now." Lucas and Matt's voices sounded in Diego's ear, acknowledging his order.

Diego took a deep breath and pushed the van door open, walking down the street towards the warehouse, towards the end.

It was chilly tonight. Diego had spent countless evenings in this neighborhood over the years and was used to the bone-numbingly cold wind that blew in off the water this time of year, but he'd learned to ignore it the way he'd ignored so many things he'd hated about that life. And he already thought of it as *that life*. Something that was all but over and done with. The fact that he was feeling the wind tonight was just another symptom of the paradigm shift that had occurred when Nora walked back into his life.

He jogged across the main street to the warehouse, not bothering to hide himself or to stay quiet once he was in view of the building. As surely as he could feel his own men's eyes on him, he knew El Jefe's men were out here as well, biding their time and relaying his location to their master. And it felt so fucking good that he no longer had to hide. He walked up the battered wooden steps and threw open the heavy metal door, which apparently no one had remembered to secure, and entered the building for what he knew would be the last time.

His footsteps echoed in the cavernous space, as did the laughing voices of the men on Salazar's crew. But as his steps drew closer to the main area, where the men were arranged around the conference table, the laughter died. Eleven pairs of eyes turned to look at him, and the disbelief on their faces was nearly comical. Had he come back sporting a white sheet with eye-holes, rattling chains and making spooky noises, the men would not have been more stunned. They'd already believed him dead, so, therefore, he must be a ghost.

He rolled his eyes and addressed them. "Never trust rumors, boys."

They exchanged uneasy glances amongst themselves, but Banyon was the one to speak. "Padre, what's going on. Did you, uh... handle the girl?"

Diego shook his head. "Tomás tried and failed. Our plans had to be put on the back burner."

Ricky swallowed. "A-and... El Jefe was okay with that?"

Diego smiled, but it wasn't friendly. "No. El Jefe had Tomás killed." A collective gasp filled the space.

"I wondered why that fucker wasn't answering his phone," Banyon said, jumping to his feet and running a hand through his hair in agitation. "Dead, Padre? Are you sure?"

Diego nodded solemnly. He'd seen the police photos and positively identified Tomás's body.

"We need to figure out a way to get his remains to his sister and his nieces," Banyon said, glaring at Diego as though waiting for a confrontation. But Diego merely nodded again.

"I'll have it taken care of. But in the meantime, we have other things to worry about."

"Like El Jefe," Ricky said nervously. His face was still mottled yellow and brown, a stark reminder of his beating a week ago.

Diego flexed his hand, noting that his own bruises had healed completely, then looked around at each of the faces turned towards him. "El Jefe decided it was time to destroy the warehouse and dismantle the entire Boston operation. You know what that means, right?"

The men looked back and forth, wide-eyed panic written on their faces, and once again Diego felt the familiar urge to guide them to safety. "They—*the authorities*—found out El Jefe's real identity," Diego continued. "It's only a matter of time before the whole thing comes crashing down. And you know how El Jefe feels about tying up loose ends."

Ricky pushed to his feet, slack-jawed with fear. "No way. What do we do?"

Diego opened his mouth to speak, but before he could, a familiar but unexpected voice echoed around the nearly-empty warehouse. "You follow orders," it said. "Right, Santiago?"

Oh, no way.

Diego spun in the direction of the voice, his hand reaching for the gun tucked into his waistband, but all around the space, echoing from the shadowy catwalk that ran around the perimeter of the second story, came the unmistakable metallic *clank* of multiple firearms being loaded simultaneously.

Cold fear settled in Diego's stomach like iron. El Jefe's men were up there, poised to shoot Padre and his crew like fish in a goddamn barrel. He had to give it to El Jefe. It was a solid fucking plan. A bunch of thugs and suspected criminals dying en masse in a shootout? The police would never question it. And then, when the building burned, how easy would it be to claim it was gang-related, one group seeking vengeance on another?

"Ah-ah-ah!" the voice warned, and Diego froze in place instantly. "Hands up, Mister Santiago. Now turn around *slowly*."

As Diego turned, he saw his men staring around wide-eyed, wondering what the fuck was going on and how the hell this stranger knew Padre's real name. Then the man stepped out of the shadows.

"Michael Darby?" Diego spat. "Fuck." Diego had known that El Jefe had spies everywhere, but he hadn't expected the bumbling FBI agent was one of them. Michael... *Miguel*. He shook his head in disbelief.

"Ah, Diego." Darby shrugged indulgently, walking in a slow circle around Diego, and extracting Diego's weapon from the back of his pants. "Don't feel too bad for not making me. I haven't been on El Jefe's payroll for long." He held the gun with a piece of fabric, the better to ensure that his prints were nowhere at the scene.

He caught a flash from the corner of his eye, a hint of movement on the balcony, and a muffled thud coming from above, but no one else seemed to notice.

"And now what? You're going to kill all of us? Make it look like we killed each other?" Diego said, stalling for time.

"You want me to do one of those villain monologues?" Darby teased, his eyes crinkling at the corners as he regarded Diego. "I'm afraid I can't oblige you. I'm hardly the criminal mastermind here. I just follow El Jefe's orders." He laughed. "And apparently so do you." Darby stepped closer, studying Diego's face. "I've gotta say, I'm surprised to see you here. You knew what this meeting tonight was. You knew you'd be walking into a bloodbath. And thanks to me, you have no backup. So why not stay home, and stay safe?"

Diego remained silent, his eyes focused on the back wall. Darby chuckled again. "Ah, I see. Savior complex, hmm? Needed to come back to help save this scum." He shook his head. "And now you'll die with them. Idiot."

Darby stepped back and tapped a comm unit in his ear. "We're in position. They're all here. Yes, even Diego." Darby smiled at him. "Yes, ma'am. I'll take care of phase one, and then we'll await your go-ahead. Five minutes. *Si*."

Darby's voice rose as he addressed the invisible men who waited in the darkness of the second story. "Shoot them all," he said in a bored voice. "Then wait for confirmation."

Banyon and Ricky ran for the dubious cover of the wooden table, while several other men ran towards the makeshift offices at the back of the warehouse. Not a single shot was fired from above.

"I said *shoot them!*" Darby demanded in frustration, turning his gaze upward, wondering why the men weren't heeding his command.

Diego smiled and stepped towards Darby. "Looks like *you're* the idiot. You were wrong, Miguel."

"Stay back!" Darby yelled, frightened now. He didn't pull a weapon, and Diego rolled his eyes. How like this arrogant prick to come to this confrontation unarmed! So fucking sure that someone else would do his work for him. "Shoot him, for fuck's sake!"

"Slay?" Diego said calmly.

Slay's voice drifted down from above. "Perimeter is secured. Darby's men have been neutralized. And Darby, you motherfucker, I will take the greatest possible joy in reporting tonight's activities to Berkley myself. Let's see how prison treats you."

Darby's face paled. "S-slater?"

"The one and only, asshole."

Darby's eyes closed. Just then, the doors to the warehouse burst open and the members of Slay's team who hadn't been taking out Darby's men on the second floor, began rounding up the members of Salazar's crew. Diego could lie and say he didn't appreciate the way one of Slay's guys threw Darby to the floor and mashed his cheek into the concrete before securing him in zip ties and leading him away, but he figured his loud laughter would have given the lie away.

Diego wandered over to the conference table, the scene of so many meetings between Padre and the crew. It was hard to believe that this whole fucking thing was really over, that tomorrow morning he'd be able to wake up next to his woman and be a whole different person than the man he'd been all these years—he'd finally be leaving Padre behind.

Slay's excited voice brought him out of his reverie. "We have confirmation! Diana Consuelos is in custody! We were able to trace the transmission from her communication with Darby and found her waiting in a restaurant a few blocks over. Local PD is on their way to secure the scene. It's time to go home!"

"Roger that, Slay." Diego glanced around the nearly empty space. "I am so ready to go home." Home… Not a place, but a person. Nora, who would always be waiting for him.

His penance was served, his demons finally contained, and he felt a curious lightness in his gut that he finally identified as… *hope*. Padre was gone forever, and now he would be Nora's daddy for the rest of his days.

Epilogue

The rays of the sun hit Nora's golden hair as Tessa tucked a curly tendril behind her sister's ear. Nora's long blonde locks hung loose about her shoulders, but thin curls framed her face. Graceful twists of gold clips studded with small white flowers adorned the simple style that made her feel fairy-like. The whole day was magical.

Today was the day she'd stand before her sister and the friends they'd forged bonds with, and pledge herself to the man she loved. Today was the day she'd become *Nora Santiago*. Standing at the back of the church as her sister adjusted her veil just one more time, she took it all in, waiting for her cue. They'd chosen one of the smallest, oldest churches in Boston, a tiny chapel founded by Italian immigrants that looked as if it could've come straight from Italy. The large, stained-glass windows filtered colored light onto the small, dark wooden benches, and paintings of winged angels and saints adorned the walls. But what caught Nora's attention wasn't the intricate details of the church, but who sat within it—every one of her adopted family members, from Slay and Allie to Dom and Heidi, along with their children ranging in age from the tiniest of the bunch, Alice and Slay's little girl nestled snug in Slay's arms, to Alice's Charlie, who now stood almost as tall as his mom. And to the right side, standing fittingly in front of a large statue of Saint Michael the archangel wielding his mighty sword, stood Nora's future husband, clad in a simple but elegant black suit, the cut accentuating his strength and lean, muscled body. He'd grown his beard longer and trimmed it. She shivered. He was strong, powerful, masculine... and all hers.

Diego shifted on his feet, his hands clasped in front of him, and she wondered if his constant need for vigilance would be something he struggled with for the rest of his life. He looked over his shoulder, scanned the crowd, shot a chin lift to Slay, and then his gaze came to the back of the church where Nora stood with Tessa. When his eyes met hers, he stilled. Her heart squeezed just a little, as Tessa took her hand. "Let's go, honey."

A small church, with fewer than two dozen witnesses present, seemed the fitting way for her to take her vows, to pledge herself to Diego, as by now it was a mere formality. She was his, and always would be.

She clasped the small bouquet of early spring flowers Tessa had fashioned for her from the wildflowers that grew in the little garden outside the kitchen window at Diego's house, which she now shared. A cool spring breeze ruffled her dress from an open window, and in the distance, a chickadee whistled and a wood thrush trilled its flute-like melody. As she entered the church, everyone stood, and she smiled to herself. It felt fitting to meet Diego amidst all of them, to stand with them as she took her vows, for she no longer stood alone. She'd made her place in the world. When she reached him, he took her hand, kissed her fingers, and tucked her by his side... right where she belonged.

WHILE ALLIE HELD her sleeping daughter, Slay got to his feet in the function room at *Cara*, and Tony clinked his glass with a fork. Slay cleared his throat, and everyone quieted. Diego took Nora's left hand in both of his and nestled them in his lap as they listened to Slay speak.

"Gonna keep this short and sweet," Slay said, his deep voice garnering everyone's attention. "Pretty sure my crew will start raiding Tony's kitchen if I don't." Laughter rang in the room, as everyone knew he referred not to the men who worked for him but his passel of kids. The laughter died down as Slay's eyes sobered. He cleared his throat. "I met Diego years ago, when he was still a punk kid from the city." His eyes twinkled. "Words can't express how happy I am to see the man he's become. I first met Nora when she was a kid, still in high school…" His voice trailed off. Everyone in the room knew that Slay met Nora for the first time when he'd helped Diego rescue her from Salazar's clutches, earning Slay a gunshot wound he still bore today. It was clear he didn't want to get into details, nor did he need to. Even the children in the room seemed to understand the significance of the moment, as they sat quietly, listening. Allie looked at them fondly, Slay looked on with pride, and Nora smiled. Some day, she and Diego would have children of their own. They'd come so far.

Slay continued. "And now in front of me, sits a brother who's forged his way as a man of honor, and a woman who's grown with grace from childhood to adulthood in front of our very eyes." He swallowed, and lifted his glass. "I know I speak for everyone in this room when I say that you've made us all proud. If any couple deserves peace and happiness, it's you two. To peace, love, and finding your happily ever after."

Cheers rang through the room and glasses clinked as Diego leaned in and whispered to Nora. "Thought he was gonna start crying and I'd have to kick his ass." She snickered, but noticed he downed his champagne quickly, no doubt swallowing the lump in his throat like she did. And as she looked about the room, at

Dom and Heidi laughing at something Matteo and Hillary were recounting, at John and Paul sliding pastries on a gleaming silver tray and speaking quietly to one another, to Elena, who fixed Blake's tie as he bounced a toddler on his knee, and Tony and Tessa, who sat watching Diego and Nora with pride, to Grace and Donnie who stood by the door refereeing the most rambunctious of the little ones, she gave thanks for how far they'd all come.

Every one of them had a story, a history, and they'd made their way.

She glanced sideways at Diego, who'd loosened his tie but still wore his white shirt unbuttoned at the collar, revealing tanned skin. God, she couldn't wait to get him home tonight.

The past few months had been a blur as Diego tidied up the last details of his investigation. El Jefe now sat in jail awaiting trial, and Nora had finally come to grips with the fact that Diana was a criminal. It killed at first, knowing the woman she'd looked up to hadn't been who she said she was. It hadn't been easy. At first she'd questioned everything, wondering how she'd failed to see the truth right in front of her. But her family, this amazing group of people who'd found and chosen each other, had rallied around to support her. They, along with the women and children she helped every day at *Centered*, reminded her that having faith in other people, choosing to find the good in them, was a gift and not a crime. It was a gift that Diego said had saved his soul.

Michael Darby was behind bars, along with El Jefe and the men in Padre's crew. Thanks to Diego and Slay's team, El Jefe's entire crime ring up and down the East coast had been unearthed and disbanded. Once she was completely sure the danger from El Jefe's crew had passed, that they could no longer harm her or her family, beautiful, resilient Camila had finally told them about how she'd been kidnapped and transported to Boston. Now, the girl had been reunited with her family, but

Nora stayed in regular contact with her, and her parents kept Nora updated on Camila's progress.

Nora had even managed to contact every one of the women from *Centered* who Diana had "relocated" to Miami, and discovered that they were still, miraculously, safe. Diana had been using them for free labor at one of the many legitimate businesses she owned in Florida, and although they'd essentially been prisoners, none of them had been physically harmed.

And Diego… he'd come a long way. He now managed to actually *sleep* at night, instead of tossing and turning and muttering to himself, always watchful, always vigilant. She no longer woke up to an empty bed while he roamed the house haunted by what troubled him, and when she woke he was instead by her side, holding onto her as if to protect her, but deep down inside, she knew that he needed her as much as she needed him.

THE CRYSTAL CLEAR water went on as far as the eye could see, blue-tinged, reflecting the red-orange rays of the setting sun.

"White sand," Diego had said. "I want white sand and cold drinks and a swanky hotel."

So white sand it was, along the crescent-shaped beach lined with palm trees of Kauna'oa Bay, Hawaii. They'd arrived after a ten-hour flight the night before, and after a good night's sleep, and a deliciously lazy morning, they were settling in for some relaxation. Nora adjusted her towel on the hot sand, leaned over, and kissed Diego's cheek. He smiled at her briefly before scanning the beach, mere habit now, as everyone he'd been trying to bring down now stood behind bars and Diego was a free man.

"Relax, Daddy," Nora said, "Just close your eyes and enjoy yourself. You've earned it."

He laid back, and she smiled to herself as he *actually closed his eyes* and rested.

It was the end of an era, but just the beginning of good things to come.

THE END

Jane Henry

USA Today bestselling author Jane Henry pens stern but loving alpha heroes, feisty heroines, and emotion-driven happily-ever-afters. She writes what she loves to read: kink with a tender touch. Jane is a hopeless romantic who lives on the East Coast with a houseful of children and her very own Prince Charming.

Don't miss these exciting titles by Jane Henry and Blushing Books!

A Thousand Yesses

Bound to You series
Begin Again, Book 1
Come Back To Me, Book 2
Complete Me, Book 3

Boston Doms Series
By Jane Henry and Maisy Archer
My Dom, Book 1
His Submissive, Book 2
Her Protector, Book 3
His Babygirl, Book 4
His Lady, Book 5
Her Hero, Book 6
My Redemption, Book 7

Anthologies

Hero Undercover
Sunstrokes

Connect with Jane Henry
janehenrywriter.blogspot.com
janehenrywriter@gmail.com

Maisy Archer

Maisy is an unabashed book nerd who has been in love with romance since reading her first Julie Garwood novel at the tender age of 12. After a decade as a technical writer, she finally made the leap into writing fiction several years ago and has never looked back. Like her other great loves - coffee, caramel, beach vacations, yoga pants, and her amazing family - her love of words has only continued to grow... in a manner inversely proportional to her love of exercise, house cleaning, and large social gatherings. She loves to hear from fellow romance lovers, and is always on the hunt for her next great read.

Don't miss these exciting titles by Jane Henry and Maisy Archer with Blushing Books!

Boston Doms Series
By Jane Henry and Maisy Archer
My Dom, Book 1
His Submissive, Book 2
Her Protector, Book 3
His Babygirl, Book 4
His Lady, Book 5
Her Hero, Book 6
My Redemption, Book 7

Anthologies
Hero Undercover
Sunstrokes

Connect with Maisy Archer
janeandmaisy.com

Blushing Books

Blushing Books is one of the oldest eBook publishers on the web. We've been running websites that publish spanking and BDSM related romance and erotica since 1999, and we have been selling eBooks since 2003. We hope you'll check out our hundreds of offerings at http://www.blushingbooks.com.

Blushing Books Newsletter

Please join the Blushing Books newsletter
to receive updates & special promotional offers.
You can also join by using your mobile phone:
Just text BLUSHING to 22828.

CPSIA information can be obtained
at www.ICGtesting.com
Printed in the USA
LVHW092303250220
648245LV00001B/57